H200

AND THE CLONE HOSPITAL MASSACRE

RHONDA DOLZAN

H200
And the Clone Hospital Massacre

First published in Australia by Rhonda Dolzan 2025
www: rhondadolzan.com

*A catalogue record for this
book is available from the
National Library of Australia*

ISBN: 978-1-7644207-0-9 (pbk)

Cover image by TheDigitalDesignDock © 2025

Typesetting and design by Publicious Book Publishing
Published in collaboration with Publicious Book Publishing
www.publicious.com.au

IN MEMORY OF ALL THOSE
MASSACRED AT BABI YAR.

Part 1 – A Clone's Life

H200 scurried home to the compound frightened it was late and that was forbidden. He had gone to his secret place, and now it was almost dark, and the heavy metal entrances would soon come down.

The terrors of the night, alone, outside the walls were making him stumble. His chest was heaving with the exertion, and a rasping hollow sound came from his lips. There would be no food for him tonight as punishment for not labouring in the vegetable area section of the community garden, which was his duty after work, only then would they be given a meal before retiring to their dormitories. As the loud thud shuddered behind him, two guards led him away to the Managers Office. They were silent. The Manager said, 'H200 this is the third time you have been late, you will be locked in a cell tonight, tomorrow you will learn your punishment. Guards take him away.' The guards led him away and locked him in, they did not say anything, and it was not expected. The next day he would have to face his fate.

R630 went to rest that night knowing that because H200 did not return on time, that she would not see him again. At least she knew why, it was the third evening he had come back late. She knew where he had been, as he had told her of his secret place while they worked in the vegetable gardens. She lived for those few stolen moments every day. They had learnt to speak quietly with their mouths open, but their lips not moving, so the keepers watching would not suspect they were talking.

In the past others had just disappeared suddenly. There had been furtive whispers amongst the women on their way home from work in the afternoons; some had overheard things at their master's business or mistress's houses during the day. Disturbing, terrible things. Tears fell down her face in her silent dormitory.

The next morning when Alison Marshall entered her study at the Southern District Labour Training School, there was a note awaiting her on her desk. It informed her that H200 would no longer be her Teacher's Aide, and to select a suitable student from her graduate class to replace him. *How annoying*, she thought. H200 had been her best graduate of two years ago, brighter than her usual students. She had arranged to go away for one week, and he would have been able to take her class for her.

When graduates left the training school, they were already allocated to their future positions in various ways depending on their capabilities, anything from housekeepers, farm labourers, to industrial workers, but she had asked he remain as her aide. Her job was helping civilized society function as it should, and it was her life's vocation. In this she was held in high regard by her superiors. Mentally making up her mind who would replace him as Teacher's Aide, Alison Marshall did not consider, even for a moment, why H200 was not coming back as he was a Clone.

Next morning, instead of walking to his job at the nearby Training School, H200 was now on the compound coach heading out with all the male workers which took them to their various places of work every day. He knew not where he was going, only that his position was grim.

The coach passed the dirt road that led to the old stone building which had been his mental refuge. It was on the side of an ancient rusting railway track, higher up on a slight embankment. The roof had collapsed long ago, and as he ran up quickly to have a look at it one day on his way home, he saw that one of the beams had pierced through the floor and he could see a light coming up from below. Peering down below through the cavity he saw an underground room with a high window which allowed the light in. Climbing down a row of metal rungs set in the wall, he sat in wonder alone, his sense of freedom of what it must be like nearly suffocated him. This magnet led him back three times. He grieved the loss of his secret place and for R630.

The coach stopped at last outside an austere double story red brick building in the old quarter of Emerald City. The driver escorted H200 to the high wood gate and rang the bell. A brass plaque on the wall said, Surgery – Dr. P. Antrami.

An attractive nurse opened the solid wood panelled gate. The driver said, 'sign here,' handed him over and drove off. Ushering him in, she closed the gate. He heard a click as she swept her hand over a metal box fixed to the wall. He followed her meekly down a long corridor past a wood staircase until she entered a room on the left of it.

'This room, and the one adjoining it,' pointing to a doorway on the other side, 'is where you will work every day. Outside is a courtyard where you will put refuse tied up in plastic bags, where they are collected every night from the back lane entrance. You do not speak to anyone outside these two work rooms, unless spoken to. You will find all cleaning equipment you will need under the sink in the next room. Clean up all that is necessary every day, ready for the doctor and myself to commence work in the evenings,' she barely paused for breath, 'two medical doctors start at 6pm, getting patients ready for surgery. Get all your meals when they tell you. These can be collected from the kitchen next door every morning when you start, and every evening when you have finished for the day. You will then go immediately to your quarters in the courtyard.' Pointing to a printed list on the wall, 'these are your duties, do you understand?'

'Yes, I do,' said H200. The nurse left.

On looking at the list, the first of these duties was to strip the beds, which were in the ward where he was now standing, put the linen into blue laundry bags kept in the cupboards in the adjoining room, ready to take to the laundry later. The second duty was to clean up the operating room next door, and put all into plastic bags also, and leave by the back gate ready for collection later. Entering the adjoining room to fetch the laundry bags he opened the door; nothing could have prepared him for what awaited him.

H200 gasped in shock, he could not breath properly. Facing him were two steel flat tables with small holes in them, covered with blood and pieces of clotty flesh. Low small steel bins were near both tables with body parts sticking out of them, all in macabre disorder. There was a sink at the back of the room, he stumbled towards it avoiding the ghastly sight, but slipping on something, falls vomiting all over the floor. He wanted to scream, but no sound came out. Finding the outside door, he stumbled through it breathing huge gasps of air to stop himself from fainting. What hell on earth had he got himself into? After a while, he cleaned his shoes at the tap there, and himself the best he could and went back. He spent the next few hours putting the dirty bed linen in bags and cleaning the ward, all the time working out in his mind how he was going to be able to cope with the next grisly task. There was no going back, instinctively he knew he had to have all done by the time the doctors arrived. He had been trained from birth to do everything asked of him, and never to question. He keeps looking at the closed door. He goes into the surgery trembling. With gloved hands and averting his eyes he placed a large bag over the first bin over the bloodied parts, turns the bin upside down and the contents fall into the bag. Trying not to look he puts the bin down and does the same with the second bin. He scrapes the pieces of bone and tissue off the tables and into the bags as well. The blood had gone into two gutters running along the sides of each table and into the holes, and from there to a gutter at the end of the tables into a pipe which went down into the floor. Placing all soiled surgical waste into the bags, tied them up and dragged the bags outside, leaving them near the back gate. Though feeling very sick he started to clean up the bloody tables, floor, sink, bowls and utensils.

Finishing before 6 o'clock, H200 quickly went to his room at the end of the courtyard, via the outside door. He entered a small windowless room with a single bed, which was covered with a warm looking rug. Opening drawers in a small bedside cupboard he finds two sets of silver-coloured pants and tops made of a very soft material. In another, two sets of underwear and socks made of the same material. One pair of silver footwear lay in the bottom drawer. Off to the side of the room was an opening where he could see a toilet, shower, and basin.

How strange it would be to be sleeping and showering alone. Though talking was limited, he always had others with him. There was a large clock on the wall showing almost 6 o'clock. H200 quickly washed his face, having no time to shower, changes into one of the silver uniforms, and slipped into his soft silver shoes that were loose fitting. Before leaving, he put his own vomit blood-stained clothes at the bottom of the shower for washing later. He gets back to the ward just in time, as he heard voices and two men identically dressed as he was, came into the room. One man was of medium build and dark, and one very pale and thin.

The larger one said, 'what is your number?'

'H200.'

'This is Uri and I'm Paul.' Going over the two rooms, and coming back said to Uri, 'he's done everything, those two will be satisfied.'

'Help us make the beds said Uri, and then you can go and take the blue bags of linen down the hall to the laundry and put the washing on. Stop on the way back at the kitchen which is next to the laundry and collect our meals'.

The washing was easy, having taken turns to do it at the compound. The machine would wash, dry and steam press everything. Entering the kitchen, an old woman was placing plastic containers on a metal tray. Two large ones, and one smaller one, and three drink cups.

'Take these back', she demanded, not looking at him. As he was going out the door, she called him back. 'Wait a minute. Where are the clothes you came with?' She looked at him coldly.

He mumbled, 'I got blood all over them and threw them in the refuse bags which are out by the back gate'.

'Are you sure?' peering at him more closely.

'Yes', he replied, *thinking why have I said this*? After another moment or two of staring, she turned her back on him, and he left with the food, knowing the larger portions would not be his.

Coming back to the ward he stopped, balancing the tray on one arm so he could open the door with the other. He heard the two men quietly talking, '….and I tell you Uri that I don't like it. That's the second one this year that doc and miss licketh doc boots say ran away. G608 looked pretty depressed, but wouldn't you be if you were one of them?'

'What do I care Paul, he was only a Clone.'

'That doesn't mean he didn't have some feelings,' replied Paul.

'You shouldn't talk like that, get you into trouble around here, you know how the doc feels about them… shhh H200's coming,' Uri warned hearing the tray rattle at the door.

After eating his small meal in the ward, and back in his room H200 had a shower, washed his thin fair hair and clothes he came in, but could still smell the blood. Some stains would not come out of his shirt, so he put it in the sink to soak, and hung his pants and underwear over the shower rail.

When they were dry, he would hide them. Why did the old woman want his clothes? Going outside and looking up, stars shone down from the dark skies. Never had he seen stars like this. Feelings of freedom came upon him again as he looked up, allowing himself to drown in it for a few minutes before shaking it off, as a dog shakes water from its fur. Looking up at the surgery there were lights shining behind the covered windows, so operations he knew were taking place inside. Terrible things were happening. Beating down panic, he knew he would have to get out of this place, somehow. But how?

The next day was the same, the next, and the next. Fear grew with each passing day. Each time Doctor Antrami came into the Ward, he stared at him intently when he thought H200 wasn't looking. He kept looking at his legs. He did this every day. There were only two ways H200 could think of to get out. One too terrifying to think about, which was to hide in one of the bags left at the back gate, but where did that go? He had never seen the gate open and what kind of truck collected the bags. Possibly the other was by way of the kitchen. He did not know if the old lady was there all day, but night would be easier and give him time to go further away. Where to go? That was the biggest hurdle of all.

On the fifth night he awoke, listened but heard nothing. What had woken him? He got up and slowly opened the door enough to put his right eye in the crack and look out. He saw the back gate was open and not only was there the two bags he had left, but now there was another. A torch was shining, H200 could see a van outside in the lane. Uri was handing the man with him a packet, who opened it and looked inside, then put it inside his jacket. They then took one bag each out through the gate. Coming back both men laboured under the weight of the other, lifting it up together taking it out through the opening. H200 closed his door gently and quickly covered his head under his rug in his bed. He had no doubts that he had seen money change hands, and a body removed from the premises. When quiet, he got up and went out to the back gate, unsuccessfully tries to open it. He also tries to climb up the wall in a few places but falls back down.

Determined to get a look at what was outside the kitchen next day, H200 decided to risk putting the washing under the stairs, run up to the landing and try and find a window overlooking the kitchen to see if it was another enclosed courtyard or a back area with possibility for any kind of escape.

When the time came, he raced up two steps at a time, his heart racing, turned left at the landing, and saw there were three rooms on the same side as the kitchen below. He went for the first door closest to him. Listening at the door he heard no sound, so he opened it and stood in shock. Doctor Antrami and his nurse were in a large double bed together. He was on his back, his left arm stretched out over the side of the bed, and she snuggled up against him, one arm around him. They were asleep. He clumsily shut the door and ran down the stairs picking up the linen on his way to the laundry. Shaking, he had forgotten why he went. Upstairs the doctor opened his eyes when he heard the door shut. Leaping up, was on the landing just in time to see H200 disappear down the corridor. Myrna sleepily called, 'what's the matter darling?'

'Nothing, go back to sleep'.

No nothing was the matter, the lad wasn't going anywhere, he had other important plans for him. His right leg was just perfect.

Doctor Antrami was coming to terms with an idea that had been formulating in his mind for some time. To use H200's right leg for his son. None of the other Clones he had operated on for various parts were the right size and build. It had been a terrible accident, speeding around the country, youth thinking they are immortal. Over-corrected on a bend, crashing into a large tree. He was lucky to be alive. A bionic leg should have been fitted, but he was refusing to have it. His mental state was becoming unstable - his wife and staff having a hard time controlling him.

He had been arguing over this issue of being lawfully allowed to use a Clone for transplanting limbs and organs for years. As far as he was concerned, they had been breeding them like any other animal, had no feelings concerning them one way or the other. His nurse was in love with him, and she would do anything for him which he used this for his own ends needing her for her surgery expertise. Transplants over the years were easier to perform with two or three professionals. If it had been as years gone by, it would not have been possible. In the meantime he hoped to influence members of the Senate in their decision for a 'NO' vote at the coming Senate sitting.

Doctor Antrami had made time in his busy schedule and was travelling on his way home. His new vehicle was handling well. It streaked along the upper road to Goolwa that towered above the other roads and allowed a much faster speed than below, his journey only taking a mere 20 minutes instead of the usual 60 from the city if on the next level down.

Anxious to see Aaron, Doctor Antrami quickly dropped off his medical kit with Clarise, one of their three Clone maids who greeted him at the door, and hastened to the large suite of rooms that his son occupied. Hearing a crash, he entered to find Aaron sprawled on the floor, his balancing apparatus on the floor with him. His father started to say, 'son, you are not strong enough yet to get up by yourself, you should have called...'

Aaron spewing forth numerous obscenities as his father helped him up, his face red with rage. 'When am I going to get my new leg? You promised me weeks ago, you don't care,' he shouted. Picking up a glass on the table next to the chair he had been placed in, threw it against a wood seat at the bottom of his bed where it smashed into pieces.

'Your leg is healing well, are you having any pain?'

Allowing his father to examine the stump that was just below the knee, he sat sulking and would not answer any of his questions. He was their only child and had been spoilt. Being cooped up for nearly three months only recently permitting one or two of his closest friends to visit him when he had been in bed covered hadn't helped. When he came back with his new leg, there must be no suspicion. 'I've got good news for you I've found a suitable leg.' After giving him the good news, went to find his wife.

Over lunch he said, 'Reema it was a terrible accident, Aaron should not have been speeding around the countryside, youth think they are immortal and crashing into that large tree, but he's lucky to be alive. We have tried to get him to use a prosthetic or bionic leg but he has flatly refused. I'm worried about his mental state, he's becoming unstable, so I have told him today that I have found a leg I can use. I want you to bring him to my surgery next week and I will perform the operation.'

'He's been spoilt for 19 years. How are you going to get Aaron a new leg? Are you going to use a Clone's leg? Who is the Clone, will he be alright afterwards, or will you leave him to die? You know this is illegal. At last, the debate is going to the Senate for a YES or NO vote whether Clones will have the same privileges as the rest of us have. If a YES vote is passed, it will be too dangerous for you to use Clones for your operations, and if a YES vote goes through you will not get anymore rich patients.'

'You have no right to be righteous,' her husband said angrily, 'you are surrounded in luxury. You know I have been arguing over this issue of being able to use Clones for transplanting limbs and organs for years. As far as I'm concerned, they have been bred like any other animal, and I have no feelings for them one way or the other. In the mean-time I am preparing for the debate, and I intend to influence the members in the Senate for their decision for a NO vote at the coming Senate sitting.'

‘I can’t stand it. Looking at all the luxury around me, I hate everything I see. I didn’t realise until now, it’s most probably all been paid for by wealthy patients. Blood money!’

Doctor Antrami goes up to Reema and shakes her roughly by the shoulders. ‘You can’t prove anything. I have never allowed you to be involved in my work. I am leaving tomorrow morning. I have business meetings with staff for our property this afternoon. Arrange a light meal for me this evening, after I’ve finished, I intend to retire as leaving very early. My nurse will be in contact with you to finalise Aaron’s admittance.’

Reema sobbing. ‘You are heartless, and I hate you!’ She runs from the room.

Clearing up a few matters concerning their property, and after enjoying his evening meal Doctor Antrami retired early. Next day he was on the way to the city just as the sun was peering over the hills to his right. Reema had been very quiet at dinner the night before making little comment while property matters had been discussed. Had she somehow found out about Myrna? He didn’t really care. They had drifted apart. There was little to keep them together except their son. When Aron was well again, he would see about getting rid of her. Passing over the old unused Currency Creek cemetery, he looked down.

During the night Reema had faced a nightmare dilemma. Who should she help, a Clone or her son? Today, she was composed, and felt secure, she was going to act on the side of right. She did not know the number or anything about the Clone her husband had chosen. Her position was nevertheless clear, she must save him. Losing his leg would mean losing his life. He would be left to bleed to death, taken and buried somewhere with other Clones and people her husband had used. Aaron had worn her out since the accident. He had always been closer to her husband they were so alike. She had lost respect for both. There was no compassion for a Clone from either of the males in her home. They were completely heartless. She decided to phone Paul as soon as her husband left.

'Paul I'm sorry to wake you, I'm desperate. I want a meeting today, just the three of us, myself, you and your father Doctor Styler. I can't talk here, one of the live-in maids has been spying on me, but during the night I had to face a nightmare decision. Who should I help, a Clone or my son? I don't know anything about the Clone whose leg my husband has chosen, but we must save him. He wants me to bring Aaron to the surgery next week.'

'I've been aware of Doctor Antrami's persistent interest in our last Clone assistant's leg, his number is H200, and of course I know of your son's accident. If he wants you to bring Aaron into the surgery next week, he must intend to transplant H200's leg to your son. I will phone my father and meet you at the usual place this afternoon.'

A meeting had been called by Reema for Paul, his father, a surgical doctor, and herself at the usual venue. They were the head of the Equal Rights Underground Organization set up to save as many Clones lives as possible and hide them. They liaised with other organizations with the same goals. They now had medical members working in all major surgical hospitals in the land. Paul knew a plan had to be put in place as soon as possible. Ignoring the upper express level, he travelled on the old South Road until he came to Myponga, turned left along a narrow road until coming to a right-hand dirt one, turning into it came to a dead end in front of a gated farm. Passing through closing the gate behind him he travelled on the only road in and out of the farm and soon reached an old timber farmhouse up on the rise of a hill on his left.

He was the last to arrive. Over a cup of tea, they made their familiar plan as before, but with a difference. 'As this patient is your son,' said Paul, 'I suspect the doctor will get Uri and his nurse to take Aaron to an upstairs room which would be ready to receive him, where he would be out of sight. I doubt there would be any others that night, as he would be totally consumed with this one operation.'

Sometimes with Uri's help Paul was able to get some of the bodies out to the back of his van where his father was waiting to cauterize the limb or wound to stop the blood flow before it was too late. Doctor Antrami was of course unaware of this and was paying Uri to leave the bodies by the back gate for someone to collect and take to various locations to dispose of them. 'Lately, these operations are becoming more frequent which is really worrying me,' said Paul, 'I am putting it down to the doctor's fear the upcoming vote will go against what he is doing, so is trying to fit in as many operations as possible. I do not get to see all the bodies, so I expect others must be going out by the back gate.'

'The doctor has become known by the wealthy who are anxious to use his greed and low morals, and the financial gains are enormous. All of which will put him in serious trouble if he is found out should the "YES" vote be carried,' said Doctor Styler.

They arranged for Paul and his father to bring H200 to the uranium mine hospital which was not far from where they were now deliberating. Many years ago, uranium had been found there.

The Government of the time had built a long building with a few bedrooms, dining area, a kitchen and amenities for the workers, but the uranium quality they mined did not match enough quantity to merit further investment and it was closed. A large parcel of land on the side of the mine was retained by the Government for regrowth of the vegetation and could not be sold. Rabbits undisturbed bred prolifically providing a valuable source of meat. Vegetable gardens provided healthy nutrition, so Clones became sturdy, and they were educated by teachers sympathetic to the cause. The trio discussed organization matters and the upcoming "YES" and "NO" senate vote.

Doctor Antrami was with Myrna in their bedroom on top of the surgery. 'My son will be coming to the surgery next week, and I am going to operate, you and Uri will assist. I will have to cut off Aaron's stump to make a clean cut and attach the Clones leg. Reema is not at all happy about this operation and is now suspicious of my work, and for the first time I am concerned about her loyalty. She was very quiet during our meal last night, which has me worried. She may have found out about us, if she has, I don't really care, we have drifted apart. There is little to keep us together except our son. When Aaron is well again, I am going to see about getting rid of her.'

'You know how much I love you darling. Divorce her, then we can live together, you know how much I want that, and you know you can trust me. I would do anything for you.'

'I'm seriously thinking of something more permanent, and I want all the property we own.' he said quietly.

R630 had heard of hell, and she was in it. Her previous gentle employer had died, and she now had a new employer, a Mrs Kresac who was intoxicated again, dangerous to be near, and there was no one to turn to. Mr Kresac came home early sometimes before the coach passed the house to collect her, and she entered another hell as he pulled her into whatever corner of the house was furthest away from his wife and brutally raped her. She had been told of these things on the way home on the coach when she was still working for her former employer, a nice old lady who had died. Some of those girls and a woman had reported the treatment to their Compound Manager, but nothing was ever done about it. Some were not seen again which made them all afraid. Blue marks on R630's neck showed her employers wrath already that day, and she could hear her throwing things around.

'Get in here you little piece of filth, and clean up this mess, or get a thrashing.'

Fear gripped her as she collected a broom and dustpan from the laundry. Soon as she was inside the door the deranged woman grabbed her by the hair and pulled her violently into the room. 'Why have you taken so long?' she demanded, throwing her over the room where she collided into a chair. R630 cleaned up quickly going around her employer who was drinking out of a bottle. Goes back into the laundry at the back of the house to get away from her, is accosted by Mr Kresac who had come home early. He grabs her, closes the door and violently rapes her. She tries to scream but no sound come from her mouth.

'You make one sound, you slut, and I'll kill you.' When he has finished, he threw her away like a piece of trash. He quickly adjusted his trousers. 'My wife is calling for you, what are you waiting for? Keep your mouth shut. Not a word to anyone, you hear. One word and you will be so sorry, you will wish you had never been created.'

Hardly standing, she blindly stumbles into the hall where Mrs Kresac is waiting for her, this time she throws her over the hallway where she hits her head on the corner of a hall table and blacks out.

Awakening in pain she found herself in her dormitory, all the women were getting ready to go down to breakfast and out to work. R801 who slept next to her whispered in her ear that her employer had told the coach driver the evening before to come into their house and collect her, saying she had slipped on steps going out the back of their house and was unconscious.

The Compound Manager was on his phone in his office. 'Yes, Mrs Kresac, I have noted everything down you have related to me re R630's conduct, and I must apologise for the problems you have had with this Clone. She previously worked for an elderly lady who never gave any complaint. I will send you another in the next day or so. I must say that on looking at our records it seems that the last Clone assigned to your household you reported as a run-away. She disappeared and didn't come back. No, no, I'm sure there was no fault on your part. I will be in touch when I can give you details on your new Clone help. Goodbye.'

His assistant came into his office, 'there a Mr Kresac here to speak to you Manager. He's very agitated.'

'Does he have an appointment?'

'No, it's very irregular, but he insists on seeing you.'

Mr Kresac burst into the Managers office. 'I insist you return R630 to assist my wife today. My wife is not well, and this Clone has been hardworking and exemplary in her behaviour. We cannot do without her.'

The Compound Manager is very surprised, 'I must notify you that Clone R630 has not recovered sufficiently for work, she has been removed to the Clone Assessment Clinic Mr Kresac.' Concern covers his face when he hears this news. He turns and abruptly leaves the Managers office without saying a word.

The Manager calls his assistant into his office. 'R630 is the second Clone assigned to the Kresac household in the last few months. Last one disappeared and didn't come back, and the current one has definitely been injured, and her mental state is not sound. The Clone definitely needed to be assessed to see if she can continue to function to be able to work.' He thought for a moment. 'I think it prudent that we send a report to The Clones Affairs Department. Mrs Kresac said she didn't do her work to her satisfaction, and her husband says her work is exemplary. Something not right here. Personally, I don't care what happens to them, but there are repercussions for not reporting physical abuse of Clones in employment. By sending in our report, it will give the Clones Affairs Department the responsibility of following up the matter.'

Doctor Styler at the Clone Assessment Clinic looked at the list of new arrivals allotted to him. There were three. Any that were deemed mentally unfit had to be assessed by him. Some might still be useful in some capacity. Others would stare at nothing with cold vacant eyes. These had no desire to live as they were broken and had given up. Their traumas too difficult to bear. Of the latter, he was authorized to give such Clones a terminal injection and they were cremated. For some there was no other choice.

R630 was a difficult decision. Numerous wounds old and new showed she had been physically abused and she was pregnant. Of the latter, the offender, if found and proved guilty would be severely deal with, as cohabitation of humans and Clones was strictly forbidden. The resulting child would not be allowed to live. Could he save the mother? What about the child, it would have to be aborted? What would that do to her mentally?

Doctor Styler recorded her death, reason given as not mentally fit for any work, but did not mention the pregnancy. When he was off duty, he took her number off the cremation list, and smuggled her out wrapped in a blanket, putting her gently into the back of his car and taking her to the secret mine site. He had done the same for others, the records showed they were no longer living, and many at the mine were nursed back to sanity and life. Those that did not were humanely cared for in a separate section of the hospital.

Next day Doctor Styler was confronted by an excitable night Sister who had been awaiting him before going off duty. He heard the astonishing news that a man who claimed to be the employer of R630 one of their admitted Clones, had demanded she be returned to her employment. 'He was informed of the protocol of assessed Clones found fit to work, they were first released to the Compound Manager from where they came from, and that Manager decided their future employment after reading the Clinic's notes on their physical and mental condition,' she said, 'but being informed of this, the man went into a terrible rage and forced his way into the female ward and was looking in every bed until he was overpowered by our Clinic's two security officers that are permanently stationed here at the premises. The staff looked up our Clone records, and found her on our termination list, and the man was informed of her demise.' The Sister gathered her coat and bag ready to leave, very pleased at the impact her story was having on the listener. In parting she said, 'and the most extraordinary thing happened Doctor, when he was told that she had been put down, he immediately became calm and left without a word. In all my years here, I have never experienced such an unusual incident.'

On her leaving Doctor Styler who had been deep in thought throughout the related account, knew without doubt that the man was the father of

R630's unborn child. The security department would have taken his identity from him when he was apprehended, so he would get a copy of the security report when no one in their office. It all depended on the important forthcoming vote, and if it was a 'YES' vote he was determined this man would be made accountable for his crimes, knowing now how she had received her wounds. He hoped she would tell her story.

When at his mine office at the hospital Doctor Styler pulled out a folder from an old-fashioned filing cabinet and placed inside the copy of the man's security report which had identified him as a Mr Kresac. He dared not put these records on his electronic system, as the authorities could access his work. The files were becoming larger by the week, and the first of Doctor Antrami's the biggest. R630 was now receiving the best medical care but his dilemma was, 'what to do about the baby?' He had not realized he spoke aloud and jumped at the reply.

'What baby, what have you been up to?' He had been foolish and was relieved to see Reema at the door looking at her friend puzzled.

'I don't dare put these records on my electronic system at work. I've just put in the story of R630, she is now receiving medical care, but she has been terribly abused by her employers, the Kresacs, and I have solid good evidence that Mr Kresac has raped her multiple times by the injuries she has sustained. I am determined he will be accountable for his crimes now I know how she received her wounds. I hope when the times comes, she will tell her story. She is now pregnant!'

'Pregnant!' said Reema.

'I don't want to abort the baby it goes against everything we are trying to do. We are saving life not taking it. I'm so undecided and tired. I will wait and see if her mental state recovers, before making a decision on what to do.'

Reema was very stressed. 'I don't want you to abort the baby, but madness not doing so. What a terrible decision you have to make. When will this madness end?'

Doctor Styler goes to see his friend Doctor Damus on the day of the Senate Debate. Doctor Damus had a pile of folders and papers in his hands. 'This is one of the most important days of my life Richard, I have prepared my case thoroughly, a ruling is going to be made today, a YES or NO decision. I'm going over my presentation before going in to present my case to the Senate, if YES, they will have full rights granted and be entitled to share the laws and privileges that our society enjoys. A NO vote will bring no change.'

'I know you are heading the debate for a YES vote, and Doctor Antrami is speaking for the NO vote. Society is very split on this issue there are passionate views on both sides.' He was looking worried. 'We are both aware that Army Clones are being given illegal substances making them stronger with the intention of placing them at the forefront of battle and suicide missions.'

'Yes, I know. There are also one or two other like-minded professionals speaking today if required, but I feel that my reputation and status will ensure that a verdict of a YES vote the best possible outcome.'

Inside the courtroom twenty elders of the Senate come in, they glide over the translucent crystal floor, the hems of their long white robes mirrored in the shine as they step up onto the dais, placing themselves in unison on the semi-curved green cushion, as a curved table came forward in front of them. They were ready.

The debate for the NO voted started, and Doctor Damus did not look up until his arch-rival Doctor Antrami walks up to the lectern to speak. As his voice flowed soothingly over the room all felt the correctness and order of things as he spoke. 'Senate members – let us ease our minds and consciences, - we have done well by the Clones. We have created them, manufactured them so to speak. Do we not have the right therefore to use this being as we wish? Of course not! We are civilized, caring, thinking people. We have produced the Clone and because they have low intelligence have given them work so they may live in comfort. Live without worries and responsibilities. They are educated for three years. We have found beyond that they cannot cope. They are not illiterate as they can read and write. They are given useful work at any position within the limits of their intelligence. If a Clone dies, why is it wrong to use their limbs or organs, when we humans do the same ourselves?' The crowd nod their assent, he hurriedly moves on. 'To hear people say, they feel the same as we do, is ridiculous! Honoured Senate Members, have you ever seen a Clone laugh or smile? I think not, the element of humour is missing. If Clones cry, I have never seen it.'

Doctor Damus looking concerned, feels the sentiment of the Senate and the crowd slipping from him when at last he sat down with a look of triumphal arrogance.

Doctor Damus speaking for the YES vote approached the lectern that was on the left of the Senate members, facing those of the gallery and

Press. The burden of the world's conscience was on his shoulders, the agony showed on his face. He quietly said to himself, *'Eternal Creator, let this day end with the dignity of the human race intact.'* He started slowly. 'The struggle for the supremacy of good over evil has been constant and never ending. What value human life? Today is a day that will go down in history, and the decision we make known to all men.' He paused, 'Medical science had our survival at stake when it cloned animals, solving serious food shortages, and interfering with other foods to increase production, and overuse of drugs has meant fewer children now being born in the womb. Many of our race are sterile.' There was a longer pause. 'Members of the Senate we have always believed that human life was sacred and precious. We created Clones. Now they are being treated without any regard, given menial work to do – what we don't like to do ourselves. Now we have become dependent on Clones to do all menial tasks, at home, in industry, in our gardens and now in our military. They have never been simulated into our society or allowed to vote. Members of the Senate, the word 'human' is the keyword today. You decide today whether Clones are human, with all the rights we have. I ask you to say that they are. They feel, have emotions the same as ours. They are lethargic because they work hard all day and are not fed correctly. Herded out to the outskirts of our cities after a meagre education to grow our food late in the afternoons, which they are not allowed to eat after a long hard day. Three years education is not enough. It is sufficient to read and write, to do the manual tasks we set them. Perhaps we are afraid of them and want to keep them at this level for our own convenience.' Murmurs came from the onlookers in the gallery. 'How could we have let this happen? Our civilization is going backwards not forward. Not only do we almost starve them, keep them stupid and abuse them, but now we want to sink even further by having them stripped of the right to be called human. I am going to ask the Senate these questions,' he pauses, and has a drink of water. 'How are Clones placed in your minds? Do you think of them as human? Sub human?... Inferior human?... Usable human?...' His voice rose to a high pitch. 'Perhaps disposable human… So we can mutilate them, so we can use their limbs and organs, so we…'

An uproar erupts from the crowded room, including one or two senate members. People start arguing with the next person near them. Arguments start between the viewers and the media. Doctor Damus cannot be heard, and it is not until some order is restored that it is noticed he is no longer on his feet. A group is gathering around his body slumped over the lectern. His heart giving out for this decision which meant life itself. The decision would not be given that day.

Doctor Styler was talking at a meeting at the old farmhouse. 'We three are the head of the Equal Rights Underground Organization set up to save as many Clones as possible that are in danger. I am proud to say we now not only liaise with other organizations with same goals but now have other medical members working in all major hospitals in this State, but the three of us are in an insufferable position caused by the death of Doctor Damus. The YES vote we so fervently hoped for is now delayed, which means we have to carry on this work until a decision is made by the Senate, or a date set for another YES or NO debate.'

'Dad we just have to carry on. I had hoped the YES vote would save H200's leg. I will try to smuggle H200 out of the surgery, but it will be difficult. It might mean I will have to leave with him. Dad, if I'm not successful, you just wait outside in the van, I will stop the blood flow best I can afterwards and sneak him out to you soon as possible. The doctor and our nurse won't hang around after the operation as their whole attention will be taken up with Aaron. Uri will see me take him away, but he won't say anything, he thinks I'm crazy to care.'

'Let's hope we will be in time son if that happens.'

'We will be going to the hospital we have set up in the old disused uranium mine which is up the track from here, as he will need the hospital if he is going to have any chance at all. Thank goodness the Government thought they had quality uranium here and built the mine, but there was not enough quantity here to merit further investment and was closed.'

'Yes', said Reema, 'and the large parcel of land on the side of the mine was retained by the Government for regrowth of the vegetation and cannot be sold. No-one ever comes to have a look, nothing to see, but rabbits undisturbed have bred prolifically providing a valuable source of meat. Thank goodness I have all our farm area not far away as well, so can grow vegetables for the hospital. It's all worked very well, but the situation is becoming increasingly difficult as we are becoming over-crowded, we need more space, it was only meant to be temporary. The vote decision has taken so long. The underground war is never ending.'

'Yes, it has,' said Doctor Styler, 'and we are going to have to think where we are going to send the Clones that have recovered, not all have lost a limb or organ. A lot are suffering from mental problems from being abused. We must organise somewhere where they can go and start a new life where no one knows where they came from. In the meantime, at least we have a few teachers that are sympathetic to the cause and spend time here, so their education has improved, which keeps them occupied and useful, so now they can help with looking after the others.'

H200's dark depression had set over him like a fog, he is not doing his work properly. He is sure his life is in danger. It is evening, he has his meal in front of him but is not eating. Doctor Antrami walks up behind him and gives him a sharp slap over his head. 'What's wrong with you? You haven't cleaned up the surgery tables properly. Do them again thoroughly do you hear?' When H200 goes next door, he puts something in his drink. H200 does not know that Aaron is already installed in one of the rooms on the top floor further along the landing. Uri finishes his evening meal, leaves the room and goes upstairs. H200 occupied by his own fears, does not notice, and has not touched his evening meal, which is still in front of him, but has his drink.

When Paul sees Uri go upstairs, he follows him and listens at the door of the spare room where he hears voices.

Aaron is frightened, 'I feel scared dad.'

'Don't worry Aaron, everything will be alright, it won't be long now, soon you will wake up with a nice new leg.'

Outside in the courtyard by the back gate H200 is vomiting as he gets into a large blue bag with some body parts in it. He starts to yawn.

Paul comes back down quickly to the ward to get H200 to take him away to safety but can't find him anywhere. He goes from room to room looking under the beds and in the larger cupboards, also out to his room.

Aaron is brought into the operating room by a side door and put on the table being prepared for the operation. Doctor Antrami goes into the ward. 'Paul go get H200, the drug I put in his drink should have worked by now, pick him up and carry him back into the surgery.'

'I have looked everywhere, he is nowhere to be found, I have searched downstairs, in his room and the courtyard. I can't understand it, he can't have vanished!'

'Paul, go upstairs and look through all the wardrobes and cupboards up there, he must be somewhere, he couldn't have got away to the outside.' Doctor Antrami goes outside the back door, and he stands contemplating the back yard, looking all over with a searching gaze. He walks over to the bags left by the back gate, and he opens one and then the other. He motions Uri to come forward where he sees H200 inside one bag blood stained and unconscious.

When Paul arrives back in the ward, he realizes H200 is in the surgery, and he is too late. He wanders around the ward in torment.

Eventually Uri comes into the ward to get some pillows and bed linen. 'What's the matter with you, why are you affected by this operation. We have been through others?'

'I feel so helpless Uri, I can't take this anymore. If only the YES vote had gone through. I have to tell you that my father is waiting outside in my van. We are going to try and save H200 and take him to safety.'

'Well, you can go and get him now, Aaron has been taken upstairs, there is no one in the surgery.'

A few weeks after the operation Aaron was going home. His father was pleased. Not only was the leg working perfectly, but his son's temper also had mellowed. Reema was coming to the city that day to do some shopping and would collect him on her way home. The relationship with his wife was becoming more strained. She had made several references to what had become of the Clone whose limb he had used, and that someone could report his activities, which would mean exile or imprisonment.

'Sounds like a veiled threat,' said Myrna when she heard this. 'She's not your confidant, just how much does she know? Can you trust her silence?'

It came to Doctor Antrami once more to get rid of her. Permanently. Killing her would be easy as would be burying her body on his large property. No one would ever find her. How to explain her disappearance? A plan started to emerge. He would bring his nurse down to his house and install her there in the pretence of the need of physiotherapy care for Aaron, making no secret of his infidelity by sharing his bedroom with her. Then he could set the stage. There would be arguments which he would make sure were loud and frequent, so the maids and his son heard every word. Myrna was besotted with him and often mentioned living together which was getting on his nerves. She would help him. Household staff would think Reema had packed up and left him when found that some of her clothes and personal belonging were gone. The suitcase with her belongings would be buried with her. When asked, he would say that he had no idea where she was. Aaron would not care as they were not close. Reema had no relatives, or very close friends that he knew of that would pester him for information. Money would have to come out of her account. All must be well thought out and planned. There was no hurry.

It seemed very opportune when he was approached by a very wealthy man who was now sitting in his office. 'Don't give me your name, it is very fortunate that you have made contact with me at this time, as because of the NO vote not forthcoming as I expected, my position is becoming uncertain, so I have decided to retire. I was intending to close the surgery down by the end of the month.'

The unnamed client said, 'I hope then I can persuade you to do this one more operation before you retire.' I am a very wealthy man Doctor Antrami, and I love my wife very much. I will pay you anything you ask if you will give her a new arm. Any amount, just name the price.'

'I am sure we can come to a very mutual agreement on the fee, that is not the problem. The problem is I will need to make sure I have another suitable arm for replacement. This is something that sometimes can take some time to arrange.' Doctor Antrami suddenly stopped, as he had a sudden incredible idea. 'I think I might be able to help you sooner than I thought, is your wife a very slight to medium build?'

The Client passes over some photos. 'Why yes doctor she is of medium build. I took the liberty of taking quite a few close-up photos of her arm and body with measurements. Will these photos help? I can of course bring her in here to the surgery to see you if necessary, but she is very fragile since she had her car accident. Her nerves are shattered, and she is in constant pain.'

'I will let you know. I may need her to come in. She can come upstairs to a comfortable room up there as no one must see her.'

'And the fee? I can arrange to withdraw smaller amounts from more than one source over the next week in case it causes my accountant to query it. It's none of his business, but you won't want any attention drawn towards you. How do you want to be paid and how much?'

'I want one million dollars for the operation and body disposal costs, and I want it in cash.'

The client calmly stated, 'you shall have it.'

When Doctor Antrami was with his nurse Myrna in their bedroom upstairs that evening, he told her his plan of preparing the scene at his home so he could murder his wife. 'Myrna, fate has taken a step in my direction. I have been approached by a very wealthy man today who is willing to pay me my one million dollar fee I asked for, to give his wife a new arm. She was in a terrible accident recently. At first, I was going to refuse, then I realised seeing the photos of the patient, why bother, when I have a suitable substitute already. Reema is going to die anyway, I might as well use her body before killing her. I have become extremely wealthy in this line of business the last few years this will be the climax. I can look forward to my retirement in style.'

'*Our retirement in style*' thought Myrna.

Later in the week in the early evening, Doctor Antrami with his plan in place, forcefully gives a gagged, violent struggling Reema an injection with Myrna's help at their home to quieten her down so they can take her into his surgery in the city.

In the doctor's surgery Paul is wondering why the doctor has been so nervy and volatile during the week. 'Uri, he's acting the same way as he did when preparing for Aaron's operation. Do you know why this is?'

Uri nastily answers, 'why ask me? I don't know everything. Find out for yourself.'

Myrna calls from the bottom of the hall stairs. 'Uri you are wanted upstairs,' so he leaves the ward. Paul starts to feel uneasy and paces up and down the ward. Uri looks very disturbed when he returns.

'I was relieved when the doctor said our services would no longer be required due to his retiring to the country. We were given three weeks notice because the surgery is going to be sold. Now I'm feeling very anxious Uri, it's not like you to be so short tempered with me. What's wrong, you've got to tell me?'

Uri stumbles and sits down. 'It's Reema!'

'What about Reema, tell me?'

'Doctor brought her in late this afternoon unconscious with a drug patch on. Myrna has just placed on her another drug patch to make sure she stays thar way. He told me to put another woman waiting there into the surgery onto the operating table, and to get her ready which I've just done. I went through the side door so you didn't see us. They will both be down soon. When ready, they want us to go and get Reema and bring her down to the surgery. What shall we do Paul, what shall we do? Reema isn't a Clone, he is going to operate on her and expects me to help. He is going to murder his own wife!'

Paul is desperately trying to get himself under control. 'We must save her Uri. We can't let this happen, as soon as we are told they are ready, we will both go up and collect her and take her out to my van. I will look after her. I will not be coming back.'

'I won't be coming back to this bastard either said Uri. What can he do? Nothing. I know too much. Better make ourselves look busy when Myrna comes to get us.'

Myrna comes out briefly to gesture with a pointed finger upwards towards the ceiling.

Upstairs they cover and carefully lift Reema out of the room and go down the stairs. They hear the middle door of the surgery open. Doctor Antrami calls out, 'Uri, Paul, get a move on, and be quick about it. We are waiting.' He walks into the ward and sees them leaving, he rushes out after them. The door of the van is still open, with Uri holding Reema as the van moves off dragging Doctor Antrami along until he lets go and falls to the ground.

Paul stops at Uri's apartment. 'Wait for me Paul. I won't be long. I need you to drop me off at the Express Entrance at the Airport. I've decided I'm going as far north as I possibly can by Air Express.' While Paul waits for Uri to hastily pack a suitcase, he gets out to make Reema comfortable and closes the van door. At the Air Express entrance Paul and Uri look at each other for a few minutes in a wordless goodbye.

Two weeks later Reema is at the mine hospital with Doctor Styler who says smiling, 'it's wonderful to see you looking so well and happy.'

'It's wonderful being so useful. I'm enjoying my duties looking after sick Clones in my ward here at the hospital and being part of a community that's committed to caring for each other. My hopes and dreams for the future have returned Doctor Styler. I believe, because of his work, my husband will be punished and sentenced to a long jail term. I will get all our property. I have decided I will sell everything and take all the money and will go as far away from here as I can where I will buy land and set up a community for Clones, where they can live in peace and away from persecution.'

'Sounds a wonderful dream Reema, it would be easier if the YES vote would come through. I heard there may be a decision coming very soon.'

'Why don't you come with me?'

'My work is here Reema, there is so much to be done, especially if helping our Government to set up a New Order if the YES vote is cast. New laws will come in to protect Clones, this inhumanity must never happen again.'

'There are two dark clouds hovering over me at this time Doctor Styler. On my daily rounds I have noticed something disturbing. A moral problem. There are now a number of humans at the hospital helping Clones, as well as those

Clones who are now well enough to work in various sections of the hospital, and I can see love developing between a few, even though it is forbidden for the two groups to marry or copulate. I can see deep feelings and relationships forming even though they try to hide their true feelings. Besides that, I know of course R630 is pregnant, and that you are experiencing serious ethical difficulty on how to proceed in her case.'

The three members of the Clone Equal Rights Organization were having their weekly review of patients when Paul brought up H200's case. 'This Clone is very special to me,' concern sounding in his voice, 'his stump is now healing well, but his mind is not.'

'Do you think he has given up son,' said Doctor Styler with sympathy?'

'Yes, I have to say I do dad, I just wish I could think of something that would bring him around,' he paused and then continued, 'a couple of evenings ago I was urgently summoned to another patient in his ward, and as I passed his bed, he was thrashing around his bed calling out, 'R630. R630.' Thinking this could be helpful to know who this was, went to see him next day, but he just stared at me as usual, and would not say anything, so am completely at a loss to know what to do. The authorities might be looking for me, as goodness knows what Doctor Antrami has told them since we rescued you Reema, so can't make any enquiries at the Registrar of Clones Department to find out.'

Both Reema and Dr Styler cried out in unison.

'We know who it is, *we know who she is*!'

Taking care and time to make sure that R630 was nicely attired, and her hair combed, Reema took her into H200 who was sitting in a chair by his bed. She placed R630 in a chair next to him, then joined Paul and Doctor Styler who were standing back by the door. In unison the pair looked at each other, held out their arms, touched each other and held hands for the first time.

Emerald City flashed the important news over all private and commercial news channels, that the 'YES' vote was passed after careful deliberation by the High Senate. New laws to be passed.

Scrutiny to take effect immediately of all records at the following venues:

Hospitals
Doctor's surgeries
Military HQ and bases

Clone Camp Managers
Clone Assessment Clinics
Government Clone Vegetable Farms
Clones can have Numbers changed for Names on the Official Register if desired.
They are to be given respect and rightful place in our community.

Doctor Antrami was in his office at his home in front of his safe. He puts wads of cash and gold coins in a bag. Checks his Air Express tickets, puts them in his inside top jacket pocket. He picks up his phone and connects to Aaron's rooms. 'Aaron I'm leaving the country. I want you to come to my office, I need to explain to you what I have arranged for you.'

Aaron walks into the office with a limp, with the aid of a cane. 'Walking out on me dad, why can't I go with you?'

'Aaron, all my plans are in place, my wealth has already been transferred to other countries for safety, as insurance against such a day as this. I have left everything to you, it's all in your name as I can easily replace it. I'm travelling light, just a few essentials, plenty of cash and some investment gold coins I have collected over the years. Later I will give you the choice of joining me if you want to when things settle down and it's safe.'

He pointed to a box on his desk. 'I have left all the things you need to know on my desk in that box there, which is yours now, you will find a lawyer's particulars inside it who will help you take care of everything. You are going to have to grow up Aaron and take some responsibilities which will be hard for you. I have put aside all the wages for the staff for the next five years, giving you time to learn. It will be up to you. You will either sink or swim.' He gives his son a warm hug, picks up his valise and bulging bag and goes towards the door. The door opens before he reaches it, and three men are standing there. All straight faced and solemn. 'Doctor Antrami, you are under arrest.'

Part 2 – Clone Hospital Massacre

Arianna felt the pain, and was on the ground face down, blood streaming down on the ground from her face, before she knew what had hit her. No one came to her rescue. For a few minutes she just lay there, then struggles up on all fours like an injured animal. She saw the weapon used, a large lump of jagged concrete with her blood on it.

At last, standing up she looked around for help, but the street was totally deserted. Slowly she regained her balance and carefully went on walking towards her home which was at the end of the street. She goes through the front gate to the front door, and fumbled in her bag for her door key, gave up, banged on the door and pressed the doorbell. Her mother opened the door and screamed bringing her father hurriedly to her aid. Lifting his daughter up carried her into the kitchen gently placing her on a chair. Her mother in shock was just staring at her, until her husband said, 'get warm water and a towel woman and clean your daughters face.'

Arianna was in her warm bed, her face bandaged, she could hear her mother talking to her father, and to her older brother Jax, and sister Trace who had come home from work. 'Who could have done such a terrible thing to an innocent child?'

She heard her brother say. 'A man was yelling at me on the bus on my way home saying his son couldn't find a job, and I had taken his son's job away from him. I moved as far away as I could and didn't answer him.'

Trace her sister started to cry, 'what's the matter dear,' her mother sounded terribly upset.

'Darla my best friend at work, wouldn't speak to me today. I was very hurt, and asked her what I had done? She replied, my mother and father said I'm not allowed to talk to you anymore. But why? I asked. Because your parents are both Clones,' she replied. Some of the other staff have avoided me the last few weeks as well. The way they look at me mother, I feel afraid.'

John Hislop was going into his local hotel. He didn't like Clones. Particularly this one he saw getting out of a modern red car walking up the street. He didn't like the way he was dressed up all nice, didn't like the fact he drove a nice fast car, and he was a lawyer. Worst of all he particularly didn't like the fact that he had a shop in the main street next to a few other businesses owned by Clones. He screwed up his eyes and spat on the pavement. He goes back onto the road, and goes up to the car, and puts the palm of one hand lovingly on it and walks around the car with his hand still on the car. Looks in the office window and sees Emmitt Benson the lawyer busy at his desk. He spits on the ground again, goes back to the Huxley Hotel and goes in. He was known for his bad temper and moods, his two mates standing at the bar could see how he looked and hastily ordered him a drink. 'What's the matter now John,' said Jake taking his partially empty beer glass off the bar, and headed for a table near the front window, the others followed him, all sat down.

'It's that lawyer Clone from down the street, I hate his guts. He goes around all dressed up, shows off in that flash red car of his, and he wouldn't even give my son Clive a job.'

'What sort of job? Clive's no office worker,' said Ed.

'Course not stupid! But he's a good worker, and as this lawyer lives in a large house with a decent sized garden and lawn, thought he could get some extra work, but he turned him down. Said he already hired someone to do the work,' he drank some beer, 'and guess who got the job, a bloody Clone. That's the way it goes these days, they stick together.'

'Too many of them here, seems more coming every week,' said Ed.

'I reckon we should have a little public meeting, what do think? Bout time someone did something about this. I'll get the word around when I go round to the other towns doing my deliveries in the next couple of weeks, what do you say?'

'Bloody good idea,' agreed Jake and Ed simultaneously.

'See if you can rustle anymore to come to the meeting, we better not go to my home. Just all meet at the Football Club one night, as no one there now the season has ended. Now, which one of you pansies is going to have a game of darts?'

Emmitt Benson was becoming aware of tensions in the towns he serviced around Huxley. There were 12 small communities altogether, cut off for parts of the year due to heavy snowfalls. Each town was not entirely dependent on the others, and rarely got together except at sport carnivals, and Christmas time, and it had been like this since the early pioneers had trekked all the way up into the high mountains with horse and cart, which was still a favorite mode of transport. There was a train that travelled up the steep mountain as far as Huxley when the tunnel was open during the more temperate weather, which was where he worked. In the early days that was why people came here from Europe to get away from religious persecution, and other problems. He and other services went to their clients driving around the narrow mountain roads. He had been accepted by these people he had got to know, even though he was a half Clone. His mother was a Clone, his father had met her while in Sydney in the days mixed marriages of this kind were frowned upon. Growing up, he had been bullied at school as he carried some of the traits of a Clone. When he graduated from his law college, he was one of the first part Clones to do so. Having had enough of discrimination, hearing there was a position available in Huxley he decided to take it and try to make a life for himself as far away as possible from the world, and you couldn't get further away from city life than in this town in the high mountains of New South Wales. He had been tolerated at first, but as no one else was inclined to work in such an isolated town, anyone needing a lawyer or legal advice had to either go to the internet to get help, go to Sydney or to him. These days, he had acquired a good reputation and had many clients in Huxley, as well a few in each of the other smaller surrounding towns. What could not be done by phone, he visited the villages at least once a month. On the whole he was satisfied with his life, he now had a nice home, which he had acquired when it had become vacant a few months before. While he was on one of his rare visits to Sydney to see his aging parents, and to do any business they or his two siblings needed, he decided to get a better car. He considered he worked hard and deserved it. There was only one thing missing in his life, and that was the company of a good woman. He did not want to marry a Clone, as would not put upon his children what he had gone through, and he hadn't met anyone that he felt anything more than just friendship.

Mrs Carver took her daughter Adrianna to the Huxley Hospital to see their doctor as she was worried about Adrianna's eye which was swollen, red and weeping. They were sitting on one side of where she was sitting with a computer in front of her. Doctor Dana Bentlee was a middle-aged woman, she was short, had a wide waist and greying hair. Doctor Bentlee was concerned and said so. 'Mrs Carver your daughter was very lucky, if she had been hit a fraction more to the left, she might have lost her eyesight. Everything looks alright, but I think it best I send you for a scan just to make sure there's no further damage underneath. Did you report the incident?' There was silence. She looked up from writing a police report, 'you did report this?'

'No, I didn't Doctor, what is the point? They wouldn't act on it. My husband and I are thinking to move the family to one of the larger cabins built here on the hospital estate, we just don't feel safe anymore in the town.'

Doctor Bentlee handed her an envelope and a form and walked with them to the surgery door. 'Well, I have written a report, and I want you to both go to the Police Station tomorrow at the latest. Hand them my report and tell them what happened, and here is a form for your daughter's scan, scanning is done just down the hall on your right. If there should be anything of concern, I will get our receptionist to phone you to make another appointment.'

After her consulting hours were finished, she thought of how many so-called accidents she had attended in recent weeks. When she had arrived in Huxley, she changed her name from Reema to Dana, and with her doctor husband Scott Bentlee decided to pursue her dream and they purchased a large parcel of land to build a Hospital Medical Complex far away from city life and start a community where Clones could feel safe, she never dreamed that in a few years so many were coming here from far and wide to stay because of fear. It wasn't that they didn't have the space, but with so many now coming it was apparently causing trouble with the locals. Most of the fresh food they grew themselves in the warmer months, and there were plenty of workers happy and willing to work in their gardens, and they had cows and goats for milk. Any surplus was traded with the locals in exchange for goods they couldn't produce. It had all worked seamlessly so far. They had a Helipad on top of the hospital roof in need if any emergencies should occur that they could not handle. Their Helicopter was in a hanger near-by and flew once or twice a week to deliver mail, bring back same, and medical supplies. Apart from an occasional hitch, all seemed to be working splendidly. She went to speak to Scott her husband about her feelings, but looking through the glass windows in the operating room doors she could see he was still in surgery with another obstetrician dealing with a difficult birth. Every one of the medical staff she recognized even though all wore masks. Her husband was thinner than the others, with a narrow face and you could see the light grey rings around his eyes under his glasses. She planned to have a quiet dinner at home that night together, open a nice bottle of wine, and she would have a serious talk to him after tea by their warm fireplace, as the weather was getting much cooler.

That evening Dana could see her husband was very weary, but she had to get her fears out in the open. 'Scott dear, I must talk to you about a serious matter that has really made me very concerned.' He was laying back in his favorite comfortable lounge chair with his eyes closed but straightened up to look at her noting the stress in her voice.

'What is it darling? I thought you were rather tense over dinner. What's the matter?'

'Lately, I have had a few incidents, and accidents come into my surgery for treatment, that now I'm becoming certain are deliberate harmful acts against Clones. Today, I had a young girl, who coming home from school, had a jagged piece of cement thrown at her which hit her hard in the face, it landed a short distance away from one of her eyes. She was very fortunate, as if any closer she could have lost her eyesight. This is only one incident.'

'Did she see who did it?'

'No, by the time she managed to struggle to get up, there was no one in the street. She managed to walk home, and her mother brought her into the hospital. She told me that her older daughter was having trouble at her work with her co-workers, and her son was getting abused on the bus on his way home by hostile passengers saying he was taking jobs away from their families. The mother was very frightened and said she feared for their lives!'

'Well, I wasn't going to say anything to you Dana as didn't want to stress you, but there are certain things happening around me at the hospital that I don't like.' He hesitated. 'I heard from Doctor Burgess, our other obstetrician that he was told by the Principal of the hospital, that he was going to take off our list three promising trainees that we had put down to get an internship at the hospital when they graduated. These were all part Clones, and that's not all Dana, I have heard of other incidents where some patients in the wards are not allowing Clone nurses to attend to them, or even want them to give them their meals, or even clean the floors near them! Today we had to segregate the patients. Clones are now separate in their own rooms.'

'But Scott dear,' she was shocked, 'you are a part Clone!'

Scott just looked at her, she didn't like the fatalistic look her had on his face. 'Sometimes lately I despair of the human race,' he murmured.

Emmitt Benson was on his usual Sunday walk along the river which ambled along not far from the back of his property. The air was crisp fore-warning of the season changing. His dog Snipes was running along happily knowing there would be interesting smells along the way, and perhaps a rabbit to chase. Emmitt was lost in thought, oblivious to the beauty around him, trying not to think of work. He was very lonely, and thinking that before the town got snowed in, he should try to get to Sydney and socialize. He hated small talk and large gatherings, perhaps there might be a good play running he could see, or he could go to an Opera. Culture was hard to come by in Huxley. At least it would be a much needed change, his parents had been asking frequently as to when he was coming back to see them. They sounded troubled. He would arrange his work so he could get away in a week or so. His thoughts were interrupted by Snipes barking and looking up he saw a young woman sitting down on the grass near the river reading a book, or trying to, as Snipes was jumping all over her excited at having found a new friend to play with. Emmitt called his dog back and apologized, but was astonished when she quickly arose looking frightened, and was about to run away when suddenly she stopped and looking right at him said, 'thank goodness, I thought you were one of the horrible men from town, but I can see we are alike.'

Puzzled he looked at her, and immediately saw what she meant, there was unmistakable signs of a Clone in her face and figure, in fact, same as himself. She was a half Clone.

'My mother is a Clone,' she offered.

'Mine also.' He replied.

'I always come here when I can as I may not be able to when we move, and I will miss this place, it's so beautiful here, lately the only place I feel relaxed except in my home.' Not giving him a chance to say anything, she bent down to pat his dog who was still jumping up and down wanting her attention. 'My younger sister was attacked this week while walking home after school, and she was hurt badly. I've lost my best friend at work, because her parents have told her not to talk to me because one of my parents is a Clone, and my brother gets abuse on the bus travelling to and from work, from passengers saying he is taking a job away from one of the locals. So, my parents are seriously thinking to take our family to live up at the Hospital Estate Shelter for safety. Why is this happening, what have we done?'

Emmitt was quite close to her at this point trying to restrain his dog and was shocked when the young woman started to cry and stepping forward buried her head on his chest. Before he regained his composure, she lifted her head realizing what she was doing, turned and started to run away, but tripped over Snipes and fell to the ground. Helping her up he introduced himself, 'my name is Emmitt Benson. I'm a lawyer here in town, and this is my house,' waving in the direction of his home, 'are you alright?'

'Yes, yes. I'm fine thank you, my name is Trace Carver,' she turned and quickly ran away.

Emmitt felt very perplexed, and somewhat unsettled. He called out after her, 'will you be back next week?'

A light answer could be heard in the breeze. 'I might.'

Throughout the following week, the incident kept coming back to him, and he would go over it again and again as nothing like that had happened to him before. He only knew he wanted to see this girl again, she was very beautiful. *What in the hell are you doing*, he admonished himself. *You only saw her for a short time, a complete stranger, and what's worse she is part Clone, and you don't want to get involved with anyone who is a part Clone, do you? Do you want to ruin your life and everything you have worked for! What's the matter with you?*

Fate had another meeting in store for him. He was in his office in High Street when his phone rang, he picked it up and leaned back in his chair with a surprised look. 'Why yes, Mr Carver I did meet your daughter on Sunday. What can I do for you?' he listened, 'I can help you with any legal documents, when would you like to make an appointment? I can certainly make a house call.' Emmitt gets a notebook out and writes down an address. 'I will see you Friday at 10 o'clock.' He puts the phone down, and stares in front of him into space.

Upon arriving at the Carver home at the appointed time Mrs Carver brought in a teapot and two cups on a tray, she poured out two cups of tea and leaves the tray. While drinking his tea Sidney explained why he wanted to see him. 'I am very worried Emmitt about the situation here in Huxley. My youngest daughter was attacked on her way home from school, my son is being abused on transport going and coming home from his job. Mazie is being hassled by one of our neighbors. My wife and I have decided to move to one of the cabins on the Hospital Estate until these worrying circumstances quieten down, if they do at all. I've asked you here as don't feel I can even go into the town at present, as there is so much bad feeling everywhere.'

'How can I help Sidney?' asked Emmitt.

'I want you to make out a new will for me, and my wife. We made one years ago not long after Mazie and I were married, and naturally things have changed since then. I want to make sure my family is protected in case anything should happen to us, everything must be legal concerning our home, which at the moment is only in my name as

I inherited it from my father when he died. Also, I would appreciate any other advice you can offer me regarding tidying up my affairs.'

'I can certainly help with all you need Sidney, and there are other documents that should be in place such as an Enduring Power of Attorney, and you should have Advance Care Directive Forms in place as well. I would advise that your wife have the same. The two men talked for some time and Emmitt rose to leave, saying 'I will get back to you as soon as I have all the paperwork ready for you and your wife to sign.'

At that moment Trace walked in. 'I hope I'm not interrupting, would you both like more tea?'

'No, thank you Trace, I must get on.'

'I will see you to the door,' she opened the front door, and stepped outside with him. 'Thank you for coming, my father has not been sleeping well, he has been worrying about our future since so many are against us now.'

'Glad I can help. Will you come back to the river near my home next Sunday after lunch, it is very beautiful there, we could go for a walk by the river. It is very quiet and peaceful, no-one comes there.

Besides, Snipes would love to see you, he was very taken with you, he has good taste.'

Trace laughed. 'Alright then, I will see you after lunch on Sunday.' She went inside her home, and Emmitt went away trembling. He had started something, and he didn't know where it was going to lead.

Sunday came around slowly, but at last he went outside with Snipes, who was overjoyed at going out for a walk. The air had a cutting chill, snow was in the air. Emmitt has a warm coat on, the collar turned up around his neck. He looked anxiously up the path but cannot see Trace. 'Going to snow before long Snipes, we must make the most of it before we get snowed in.'

He was worried Trace might get cold but was relieved when he saw her coming to meet him wearing an apple green warm jacket, which suited her light brown hair, and she had smart black boots on. She was smiling and waving to him. He was overcome with happiness, she was so beautiful. She bent down and called Snipes to her, but the dog was already on his way delighted to be petted. How he envied his lucky dog. They talked and walked along a narrow path beside the river which was gurgling along with them as they went, the trees on both sides tall and bowed creating a cathedral roof over their heads. Eventually they turned and went back towards Emmitt's home. 'Won't you come in for some afternoon tea, it will warm us up?'

'That would be nice,' said Trace.

Over his cup of tea, as both sitting in the lounge room on comfortable armchairs, he kept looking at her and knew he was head over heels in love with this girl, he would have to accept his fate, and with it he felt a responsibility to protect her.

'Have you family here Emmitt?'

'No, my mother is a Clone, my father met her in Sydney and they live there. Their marriage was frowned upon by my father's relatives, nothing has changed. Lately I have been worried about them as they want to know when I will be coming to see them. It's been about two months since I last went there. I bought my new car while there. My father sounded worried so would like to go but had to explain what the weather is like here, and that we are totally snowed in soon for a month or two. Soon as possible I will take a trip to see them, perhaps you might like to come with me. They are getting older and would love to meet you.'

'Perhaps I might, I have never been to Sydney or anywhere else.' She became thoughtful. 'Emmitt, have you noticed any tension, or have heard of the same trouble as we are experiencing in Huxley when travelling to clients?'

'I have been aware of tensions surrounding Huxley for some time as I travel on business around the 12 smaller isolated communities not far from here. I came to Huxley to get away from this sort of nonsense.'

'Did you experience hostility when you lived in Sydney?'

'When I graduated at my law college, I was one of the first part Clones to do so. I had been bullied at school as I carry the traits of a Clone with my eyes and figure. I also faced a good deal of discrimination at college, so I decided to move away from Sydney.'

'What made you come to Huxley?'

'Hearing there was a position vacant for a lawyer here in Huxley, I decided to take it and try to make a life for myself and get away from the world as far as possible. I thought I couldn't get further away than this town in the high mountains of New South Wales. I was tolerated at first, but as no one else was inclined to work in such an isolated town, anyone needing a lawyer and couldn't do business electronically had to go either to Sydney or come to me. I have acquired a good reputation, and have many clients in Huxley, as well as a few in the other smaller surrounding towns.'

Trace got up and started viewing all the beautiful paintings on the walls around the lounge, then goes to a bookcase full of books, she browses through them. 'You have interesting books here Emmitt, I like reading too, we have something in common.'

'You can borrow as many as you like, anytime.'

'You have made yourself a very comfortable home, it's nice and cozy. It's getting late and I must be going as it gets dark very early now. Thank you for a lovely afternoon.'

'I'll drive you home.' He goes out to get his car from his garage, and helps Trace get into the car, and puts Snipes in the back.

John Hislop looks up the street when they have gone, walks up to the house, walks around it trying to open any of the doors and windows. Comes back to the wood garden seat outside near the front door, sits down and lights a cigarette.

Emmitt arriving at Trace's home, opens the door for her and watches her walk up to her front door.

She waves and smiles at him before disappearing inside. He knew deep down Trace had affected him in a way that no other woman had been able to.

Back at his home, Emmitt wipes his feet on the front door mat, looks down and sees a cigarette butt. Picks it up, smells it, puts his finger on the tip, but pulls it away quicky as is very hot and burns. He takes a few paces back to the edge of the veranda, looks around, but can't see anyone. He takes the butt inside with him.

Looking behind nearby trees, John Hislop sees Emmitt pick up the butt, laughs silently and walks away.

John Hislop and his friends had talked to quite a number of people re the Clone situation and how they felt about it, and a reasonable number of like-minded men and women had gathered together for their first meeting at the local Football Club. They had managed to get the owner of the local pub to come along, and obligingly he bought along some beer.

John Hislop called everyone to order. 'We are all here because we have something in common, that there are now too many Clones living here, and more still coming here every-day. They are taking our jobs. My boy Clive here can't get enough work, and Clones are willing to work cheaper than we can, they are under-quoting us.'

There was a loud 'hear, hear,' from around the room.

'Why shouldn't we be getting any work available before these Clones do, they are not even human. They shouldn't even be alive, I want to know what everyone else is thinking, and then we can decide what we can do about these vermin. State your name first.'

Immediately a large, short man with a shiny bald head stood up. He looks around, 'Quinton's my name, most of you know me, my wife and I, and our grandparents and their parents have lived here since the beginning of local settlement. We live in Almere one of the 12 towns that surround Huxley, and we never have, and never will like strangers coming here to live. It's bad enough putting up with the tourists that come here during the snow season to ski. We can't stand them but put up with it every year because they bring money with them to spend. We depend on that money each season, and what do you think is going to happen when they come here and see all these Clones everywhere and forced to mix with them like we are having to do. I'm telling everyone, they are not going to like it. It will have a bad effect on our way of life. I vote we get rid of them, make them leave.' Murmurs of agreement rippled through the small clubroom as he sat down.

'Thanks,' said John Hislop, 'we are all with you Quinton on this, next!'

'Sparkie speaking,' said a tall man, 'and as an electrician I get around quite a lot, and I would like to tell you something that bothered me the other day. I had put a small ad in the local rag for an apprentice, and I was working on the Hendricks place here in Huxley, when a Clone came up to me and asked if I would take him on as an assistant. He said he had been helping an odd job man in Sydney and had some know-how with electrical work before coming here with his family, and get this, said if I took him on, he would work for less wages than it would cost me to get anyone else!' He looked around the group with a horrified look on his face. 'Can you imagine! I taught him a few words I bet he hadn't heard before I can tell you. That's all I've got to say.'

'Thanks, Sparkie, this is only one of the reasons they have to go, they are undercutting our quotes and prices everywhere, it will affect our livelihoods said John Hislop.' He shouted: 'Next!'

An older grey-haired man rose to his feet saying, 'my name is Joe Waverly, and I live not far from Huxley. I'm here because I have a different problem that you, and all the people around here are going to have as well before long, and this is worse than anything, and I want to bring it to your attention.'

'Go ahead Joe,' John Hislop said in an encouraging manner. Inwardly he was very pleased at the way this first meeting was progressing, and he intended to have more until the time was right and everyone felt hatred for the Clones with the same intensity as he did. He knew to get everyone to do what he and his mates wanted, was to give everyone something to hate.

'I only found out about this a few days ago, and that is my daughter had been hiding from me the fact she had been seeing a Clone without my knowledge for a couple of months. My wife and I went out for a day to see relatives, but we came home early because my wife was not feeling well and found our daughter in bed with a Clone. Well! You can imagine how my wife and I felt when we became aware of this situation.' He looked around and felt comfort in all the sympathetic looks he was receiving. 'Naturally, we asked her about it, and the short end of the stick is, she said she had fallen in love with this mongrel. Of course, we said you are not going to see him again, and she tells us she is 18 years old and can do what she likes, and that he is a decent person, and if we don't want to meet him, she was still going on with the relationship! My wife and I were furious, and as a result our daughter is threatening to leave home and go and live with him. My wife and I are at our wits end, this whole situation is tearing our family apart. We just don't know what to do.' He sat down. Everyone could see how crushed he was, and how this situation was affecting him.

There was silence for a few minutes, John Hislop was letting the last problem sink in, it's one that none had really thought about. Inwardly he was rejoicing, but outwardly he looked angry, he cupped his hands over his smiling mouth and whispered to Clive, Ed and Jake, who were sitting next to him, 'this is going better than I expected,' finally he said, 'it's only going to get worse friends as so many more are here now.

This meeting is now finished, and I want you all to let friends, neighbors and interested people know we are planning another, but will have it upstairs in the cafeteria as a much larger room.'

For the second meeting, so many arrived that even the larger space upstairs at the Huxley football rooms was overcrowded, word had really travelled fast around the 12 small villages in the hills around Huxley. John Hislop and his two close mates could feel the angry atmosphere in the room by the loud voices coming from groups around the clubroom. Getting up, he viewed everyone but stayed quiet until everyone gradually quietened down so they could hear him speak. 'Great to see so many of you here tonight, and this meeting will remain the same as last one. We want to hear your stories why you don't want the Clones living here, and next time we meet I want to hear not your stories but ideas on what we are going to do about this problem.'

A woman rose to her feet quickly before he had even sat down, and he couldn't have been more delighted, because it was large old Bessie, a real nasty piece of work, just who he needed to stir things up to a boiling point for him. 'Most of you folk know me, my parents, grand-parents, and great-grandparents have lived in Muiden, and I don't like these Clones coming here. It's bad enough we have to put up with all the winter tourists that come up here for the ski season every year. I put up with it like everyone else because they bring money into the towns which we need to live on, but all these Clones do is take our money away from us. In Huxley they bought some hilly land that no one wanted and built a couple of shops over near the Hospital Estate to sell their surplus food they have over from their farms, and it's taking away customers from the locals.' Bessie was working herself up into a bad state, and hadn't finished, 'and I don't like their kids catching the school bus to Huxley with my grandkids. They are starting to make friends with my grandson Jimmy, and I'm bloody well sick of him saying they are nice and friendly, and his Clone friend did this, or his Clone friends did that. You know where that will end as they grow older?' She was working her way up to a fury. 'I won't have it,' she yelled. 'I've no intention of changing my life, it's going to stay the way it always has been, and nothing is going to change while I'm here. It's going to stay the same it's always been.' She sat down, breathless and red in the face.

'Hear, hear,' could be heard around the room.

It didn't take long for the next person to stand up. 'Hi everyone, it's Clay Holten here from Tilburg, I've just got one thing to say which really bothers me, and that's they don't look healthy,' he paused looking thoughtful, 'they always look kind of skinny and sick looking. They are not really human are they? Been made up in a tube in a laboratory somewhere, supposed to have been disposable for putting in front lines for the Military, and for other dangerous work. Just wanted everyone to know how I feel. I'm not happy at all and want to get rid of them out of our area altogether. They are strange and make me feel uncomfortable. That's all I have to say.' He sat down to applause.

Vance Fox, the local real estate agent stood up to have his say. 'I've had enough trouble the last few years trying to stop outsiders from buying property around here. I've even had customers sign contracts, then I don't ever get back to them, or answer their calls after they leave to go back to their own States, and then they are too far away to get back again. Most of them give up, but a few are very persistent, and I have to follow through otherwise I would get my license taken away. Lately I'm having to turn away Clones making the excuse that there is nothing for sale, but the situation is getting more difficult for me, and I'm sick to death of it. If something can be done, I for one will be damn glad of it, as I'm suffering from stress.' He sat down.

'Ok Vance, thanks for your view,' said John.' We certainly don't want this matter to get any further out of hand. Our homes will go down in value, you can be sure of that. If enough of them try to stay here we are going to lose our ski winter income as well, people won't want to come here if they see so many Clones everywhere they go when they get here for their holidays. The Clones will try to get work at the ski resorts, and families that come won't want their children socializing with them if they try to mingle after they finish work. It could cause a real problem. We will become a town of Clones, that will kill off our snow ski season.' A murmur rippled through the clubroom. 'Does anyone else want to say anything so I can close this meeting?'

‘I do,’ said another man who got up, ‘I’m Howard Slade from Leiden, and I can see my future, and that of my family going down, and looking around I see Clones becoming richer, while we are starting to struggle. Life is difficult enough with the economy as it is at present. Why should we let them take our jobs, and I have some friends that are becoming sick with worry. They’ve got to go.’ He sat down.

‘Thanks Howard, for letting us know how your family, and friends are being affected. We have a lot to think about. That’s it for tonight folks. There’s coffee and tea at the back of the room if you want to warm up before going out in the cold, or you would like to have a chat about the issues talked about tonight.’

As everyone was leaving, John Hislop asked his son Clive, and his mates Jake and Ed to stay behind to have a beer, ‘I want to talk to you.’ They all put chairs away and tidied up the room. When everyone had gone, and they were sitting down with drinks in front of them, he lowered his voice. ‘I have a friend just outside who wants to have a talk with us.’ A man walked in who they recognized immediately, he was an old mate of John’s with a criminal record.

‘Where in the hell did you come from Stormy, last I heard they locked you away and threw away the key,’ said Ed.

John quickly butted in. 'Stormy got out early on good behavior and looked me up. I have told him all about what's going on, and he thinks we have a perfect situation here that I feel we should take advantage of.' The men leaned forward to listen.

'How about giving a mate a beer,' said Stormy sitting down. When placed in front of him he said, 'you have got a perfect situation here alright. The locals hate the Clones and want to get rid of them, so I reckon they are not going to bother one bit if they are hassled or treated badly. I have a few friends who I know would be happy to come in with us and help. Firstly, we could get at them anywhere where it's nice and quiet, no one will take much notice at first. We will target the woman in twos or threes, and just stop them and take their gold jewelry, rings, earrings, bracelets, you get the idea. I bet no one will do anything about it, most of the victims will not even bother to report it as they are too afraid now. That will be the first stage of three.'

'What do you mean three stages,' asked Clive.

'Well, the second stage, I reckon we just rock up at their homes during the day, and take what we want, later could maybe even at night and get bigger stuff.'

'We could throw a couple of Molotov cocktails in businesses in the town that are owned by Clones to scare them,' said John.

'What are we going to put the stuff in,' said Ed, 'we will need a van.'

'That's not a problem,' said John. 'I have a dark spare van with no marking on it. You can use that. It's my old one but goes ok, I keep it in case my new one needs repairs.'

'What's stage three?' asked Jake.

'Not going to say just yet, until I can see how all this pans out first.' He gave a cruel laugh. 'But you want to get rid of these Clones, don't you? Just keep stirring the locals up to a very high pitch, and it will be easy. Clones since they were developed have been trained to do as they are told, they don't think for themselves very much, had everything decided for them, told where to sleep, what to eat. The next generation is more independent now, but still very passive. In the meantime, he thought to himself, *I'm going to do a little sightseeing.*

Andrew Bishop a local policeman, who worked with two others in the Police Station at Huxley always knew he wanted to be in the police force for as long he could remember, and he found his job satisfying, until the last week. He cursed under his breath, why was this happening to him? It all started a week ago as he was doing a routine drive around through the main streets when he saw two men assaulting a young female in a lane. He quickly stopped, jumped out of his police car, and running over towards them shouted to the men to stop. When they saw he was a policeman they ran off down the lane. He decided to let them go and turned to see if he could assist the woman. She was badly shaken, upset, and her leg was bleeding. 'They have too much of a start of me. I will take you up to the hospital as I can see you are hurt as your leg is bleeding. What's your name?'

'Cassie Harris. No thank you officer, I'll be alright. It looks worse than it is. I would appreciate a lift home.'

He was assisting her up a few steps to her house when an older woman opened the front door, and seeing him with the injured girl said, 'thank you officer for bringing my daughter home. Please come in.'

Cassie said, 'this is my mother, Leanne Harris.'

After she had attended to her daughter's wounds, Andrew instructed them to come to the police station the next day to make a complaint and provide a description of the two assailants. To his annoyance the young woman refused to want to make a statement of what happened, especially when Mrs Harris told him that this was the second time this had occurred in the last month and was worried about letting her daughter go out anywhere alone again.

'You must encourage your daughter Mrs Harris to make a statement otherwise these thugs will think they can get away with this sort of thing, and will keep doing it to others.'

She looked at him surprised, 'you mean you haven't worked it out officer, perhaps you had better have a good look at Cassie.' Puzzled, he looked straight at the girl, and he saw that she was very slim, and there was something about her narrow face and slight grey rings around her eyes that he had seen in other residents.

'Well, now you can see why she was attacked, she is part Clone, same as my deceased husband. There are people going around town, making accusations against Clones, blaming them for their unemployment, and almost everything else that they can think of. I even heard one woman say to my neighbor next door when I was in my garden, that she thought Clones were responsible for her bad vegetables, said they were going around at night poisoning things so the town people would have to buy vegetables from their gardens, higher up in the hills.' Her face made a grimace. 'Can you imagine anyone being so stupid? This sort of thing is just foolish ignorant gossip but getting around. It seems Clones are responsible for everything that's wrong in their lives, they have to blame someone, not themselves, and Clones are a perfect target.'

Back at work he told Jerry Nelson and Brenton Ridge his fellow officers what had happened. He was expecting righteous indignation, but didn't get any empathy for the girl, or any other Clones.

Brenton advised him, 'you had better tell that girl to get out of here, there's too many of them living here, and more coming. I can feel the animosity brewing like a volcano, it will eventually erupt, you mark my words.'

'Brenton's right Andrew,' agreed Jerry, 'tell any Clone you happen to meet, to get the hell out of here. Personally, I don't like them, that girl might be half human, but the older full Clones are freaks. Did you know they were originally just grown in a lab!'

Andrew was concerned for Cassie and her mother and decided to go and see them. They greeted him warmly and were genuinely pleased to see him. He voiced his fears for their safety. 'I personally don't understand why, but I have been told that the situation has becoming serious here in Huxley for part Clones, mainly because I think so many of them are coming here. People are becoming afraid of their way of life changing, and a threat to their livelihoods. I have become aware that there is an element of dissent in the community which has resulted in meetings being held here in Huxley, and many grievances aired by a large number of residents here, and from the surrounding small villages. This situation could explode, and I would like you to seriously consider moving out of the town until this matter becomes calmer.'

'I appreciate your concern officer.'

'My name is Andrew.'

'We do feel afraid because we are aware of what is happening Andrew, but we simply have nowhere else to live. Our families cut us off when my husband and I got married because they disapproved of our relationship. My parents have passed away some years ago. This house is all I own, and we live on Cassie's wages, which we make do with growing our own fruit and vegetables, so how would we survive? Don't worry Andrew, I promise you if things take a turn for the worse, we will both go up to the Hospital Shelter.'

'Just don't leave it to the last minute to make up your mind.'

Better alive than dead thought Andrew, he got up to leave. Cassie went with him to the front door. 'Cassie I am worried about you and your mother. Let's see how things go for the next week or two. Would you come out with me, perhaps for a light meal. I'm not familiar with what's in Huxley yet, perhaps you could suggest somewhere nice?'

'I'm not sure about a restaurant at the moment Andrew, but we could go on a picnic out to the mountains. It is getting very cold and will be snowing more soon. I know a picnic place with a covered shelter that we could go to for a nice lunch.'

'Sounds great, I need to check my roster for weekend work. I will phone you and we can make an arrangement. I will have to buy some warmer clothes as not prepared for this kind of weather.'

He was deeply troubled as to the future of these two women, he was surprised at his feelings for Cassie who said very little during the visit, who just sat and looked at him keenly and thoughtfully the whole time.

Andrew was becoming more concerned for Cassie, he would not admit his feelings to himself. He said to himself there was nothing he could do for them, he had warned them, but then he turned his thoughts around as to what he could do if the situation became explosive, and out of hand. Could he hide them? It would be difficult. He lived in half a house with only one bedroom, a small anti room, kitchen and bathroom, they would have to be very quiet at night, when the other occupant from the other side of the house came home from work. He would not be able to have anyone over. It could work for a short period of time, and when things returned to normal, they could return to their own residence.

The Huxley Mayor, Ray Kingsley, walks into the meeting room in the Huxley Town Hall, and stops to survey the room and is pleased to see most of the Councilors are in attendance. His deputy Mayor, Wayne Greyson comes up beside him and they both sit down together.

'We will not be dealing with the usual council business tonight as we have a serious matter right here at Huxley, and that is the amount of violence that is building up to explode caused by how many Clones are coming here wanting to settle in Huxley. No Minutes will be taken down. I want everyone's opinion on how we should handle this matter. I will start the debate by telling you all that I have no bad feelings towards them in our Community as long as they follow the rules of the Commonwealth same as others that live here. I have been informed there has been a meeting at the Football Clubrooms where many residents have given their views on how the Clones are affecting their way of life, and in some cases their livelihoods.'

'I think it's a disgrace Mayor the way they are being treated,' said Councilor Luella Watson. 'I have a very nice next door neighbor who came here to live here with her husband some years ago, in fact they were two of first to come here. They are very quiet, they have one son who was born here. The husband is an invalid, he has one amputated leg due to an accident, he does gardening for me and has quite a few other satisfied customers. The wife who is my friend does housework, they keep very much to themselves, they are no trouble to anyone. They insist on being called their old numbers, can't get used to using names, but the son does of course. So, I have got used to calling her husband H200, and her R630.'

'That may be Luella, said Councilor Hailee Foster, but not many came here then. Now they are arriving every week, now there are too many of them. My husband is not getting the work we used to rely on as they are undercutting his repair quote. It's starting to affect our finances badly, we are having to give up small luxuries and not go out as much, and our children can't keep up with the other children's activities which is hard on them.'

Councilor Edmund Smith said to the Mayor, 'they are creepy, I don't like them. I want you to use whatever power you have and stop them coming here.'

'And what do you suggest Edmund? I can't stop them from coming here by law. It's a free country.'

'There must be a way we can stop them buying a house surely, or getting a job,' suggested Councilor Cory Laine. 'If they can't get either, they would have to go elsewhere.'

'That's all very well, but what about those already here, they have property and work.' said Councilor Larry Davis.

Councilor Edith Ainsley was upset, 'I think it's disgusting the way some of you are talking about them. I know a few of them, some have already fled from dangerous environments, and have had their lives threatened. They have a right to live peaceful lives and be left alone.'

'Why,' said Councilor Edmund Smith, 'we have rights too, we were here first. Mayor, why can't we send out notification by the internet to suggest, just suggest mind you, that no more Clones be employed by businesses unless there are no local community residents that can fill the vacant position.'

'That's quite a sound idea Edmund. Well, what about the rest of you. Wayne, Billie, and Kelvin, we haven't heard from you yet, no use sitting on the fence with this one.'

'They are no use to us Mayor,' said the Deputy Mayor Wayne Greyson, 'anything you suggest is ok with me. Right from the start they were just invented in a lab, so they could make our lives easier. The Senate shouldn't have given them rights the same as the citizens of this country. It was working perfectly alright the way it was. Just let's make their lives as difficult as possible so they will move on.'

'Don't like them because they are making too much money,' said Councilor Billie Landry, we should be making the money that's here, not them.'

'I agree', said Councilor Kelvin Turner, 'get rid of them.'

'Alright,' said the Mayor, 'I will arrange a private meeting with our Police, our Fire Chief, Retailers Association and Real Estate Agent and see if we can come up with a law-abiding solution. All in agreement?' All hands go up, except Councilors Edith Ainsley and Luella Watson.

When all the others have gone, Wayne Greyson stops Mayor Kingsley from leaving. 'Ray we might have a solution to our problem. I have been approached by the person responsible for organizing the meeting at the Football Club. The person I spoke to reminded me that our Councilor and Mayor elections are coming up before long, and that it would be beneficial to us in keeping our positions if we pander to the community and do something about this. It would show on Voting Day.'

'I hear your point Wayne. I want to keep my position. I've got used to the perks it brings me and my family. I want to be kept out of anything planned. I must be squeaky clean do you understand?'

'I've also heard some disturbing news', said Wayne, 'that our Huxley lawyer has been getting involved with Clones in the area, and he has been asked to nominate for a position on the Council so he can represent Clones issues at Government level.'

‘This is dangerous Wayne, this sort of thinking could spread to other Councils. It’s got to stop before it goes any further. Tell your contact to do whatever he needs to, but keep me out of it.’

‘Mayor, do I have your permission to use a little of the Council Funds for bribery, money talks louder than I can. Would you also allow me to privately contact the Police, and the Fire Chief. I will contact each one individually so that no one will know the others are involved. The person in charge of the meeting intends to have more, he has a plan and has friends, most already here and causing all this trouble. He said after the problem solved all of that will stop.’

‘What are they going to do?’

‘I don’t know Mayor, and I don’t want to know. Better for us to be ignorant for our own good. He said he needs our help in organizing a concert. Oh. I almost forgot, we are going to be compensated well for our co-operation.’

Andrew had made an arrangement with Cassie and went up into the mountains on a Sunday afternoon to the picnic spot that Cassie had told him about. There was a table there and they put the food out that they had both brought along for their lunch. They felt so comfortable together, it was as though they had known each other a long time.

'What a great idea this was of yours Cassie, just to get away from the town and enjoy nature.'

Cassie laughing. 'Is that all Andrew!'

'Well, the food was great, you did a great job cooking the chicken, it was delicious.'

Cassie's head went down, she pulled her scarf out over her face. Smiling broadly Andrew sat down beside her on the bench, takes the scarf off her face and put his arms around her. 'The company was not bad either. Not bad at all.'

Cassie screwed up her pretty face, 'you are squashing me, Andrew.'

'I have to keep warm,' Andrew teased.

'You have your nice new thick jacket to keep you warm.'

'Cassie, Cassie darling,' he is overcome with love and kisses her fervently.

Andrew was feeling the animosity from his fellow police officers since he had voiced his feelings about the treatment of Clones, and they had been giving him the "cold shoulder," speaking to him only when necessary, and he was missing the cheerful banter that had existed between them previously, so was surprised when Brenton greeted him warmly the next morning when he went to work. 'Hi Andrew, how's everything with you? Have a good weekend?'

'Fine.' said Andrew cautiously.

There's a big concert being held in Huxley in a couple of weeks, and a friend of mine on the council has given me two free tickets for me and the wife to go, unfortunately I am rostered on for night duty that night, and Jerry has already got tickets to go with his wife to the concert as well. I was hoping you wouldn't mind changing shifts with me?'

'Not a problem Brenton,' said Andrew, 'glad to help.'

For the rest of the day, the men were more friendly and returned to the usual banter that Andrew had enjoyed previously. He was relieved. Perhaps things were going to improve at work after all.

Since the Council meeting Councilor Luella Watson was worried about her neighbor R630, went to see her. 'I'm becoming very concerned about you and your family dear. The Mayor called a special meeting the other night to address the issues facing people like yourself in Huxley. He brought to our attention meetings arranged by people not happy so many Clones coming here the past summer, and it's causing conflict among the locals. He believes the people responsible have brought in criminals that are causing the thefts and other brutal attacks on Clones that have been occurring. He thinks the situation is going to explode. I'm sure you are aware of what's happening. Have you discussed what you, your husband and Daniel would do if things got out of hand? Many Clones have already gone to the Hospital Shelter for safety, and I would feel happier knowing you were there as well.'

That evening H200 was talking to his wife and Daniel. 'We always knew there would be more danger for us, after what we went through in our youth, it never leaves you. That's why we made a hiding place as soon as we got here. Looks like we might be needing it soon until whatever is going to happen is over. This is a secret Daniel, not to be told to anyone. I will get things ready so we can shift at short notice.'

'I'll help you tomorrow morning dad, haven't been down there for a long time, used to play hide and seek with you when I was young. In the afternoon I promised I would go to Emmitt Benson's place to do a job at his house.'

Stormy asked John Hislop to drive him around the hills and towns while he was out working, saying he wanted to look around. While they were out, he asked John to stop the van every now and again, got out of the vehicle and was looking down into the deep gullies. After this had happened three times, John was puzzled and annoyed as his mate was holding him up, so he asked him what he was doing. 'Well, it's time I told you about stage three John, but first I want to ask you again. Do you really want this problem with the Clones to be handled permanently?'

'Course I do, stupid! You know how I feel about them.'

'Well, I have a final solution, when there are enough of them scuttling up to the hospital, we send a message up to the hospital at night saying an armed mob is on its way. That should be enough to get rid of most of night staff, they will get out of there as fast as they can. You, and a few of my mates all dressed the same and with our heads well covered will raid the hospital and the adjoining shelter, shouldn't have too much resistance. We will force any staff left into rooms and lock them up, and round the Clones up, put them in vans and take them away and kill them. If any manage to get away, we catch them knock them out or kill them and leave them in the snow until we have all the others into the vans and collect them last before we go. We don't want to leave blood anywhere, we must not get any blood inside the building, by morning the snow would be clean and white, and it would be a while before the snow melts, and any trace would be gone by then. Afterwards we would take them to the place I'm looking for, kill those not dead and throw the bodies so far down into a ravine not far from a road no one will ever find them. Initially the snow would cover the bodies, and by summer the snow would have melted, and the bodies would just shift down further and gradually decompose. Perhaps we could even throw down some dirt or lawn strips that would grow over the top when the weather got a bit better.'

John licked his lips. 'I would love that to happen, you know I loathe that lawyer, I want his house. The others could take other property.' He remained thoughtful, and Stormy let him digest the idea. 'I don't reckon anyone would say anything, they would be so glad the problem solved, and yes, we would all have to be wearing the same clothes and hoods over our heads and gloves. Those Clones remaining in the town would want to catch the first train out of Huxley that comes up here after the season. They would be too traumatized to say anything as surrounded by hatred with no one to turn to.'

'We don't want the police or anyone to get a smell of it,' said Stormy, 'we will have to think of some way of keeping them out of the way. I was thinking of a concert. No one would know anything about it until it was all over. When outsiders come here after the snow season, we will just say we don't know what happened to them. They were asked to leave etc.' He was silent for longer and Stormy was happy to sit and let his mate figure the whole thing out.

'I need to think about this some more Stormy, as not sure if we could be convicted if anyone pointed the finger at us, even if someone blabbed. We could say they were only trying to cover themselves, but I don't think we could be convicted if they can't find any bodies.'

'That's why I'm looking for a pinnacle of rocks with two large ones with a division in the middle not far from a track that we could just tip the bodies into. We will have to make sure we have covers in our trucks and make sure nothing is left, all must be thrown down with them,' said Stormy.

'Well, why didn't you say so in the beginning, you idiot, I know just the place, and after I've finished my next job, I will take you there. You had better get into the back of the van, don't want anyone seeing you with me, they might remember it later.

We better not meet in the pub only at my house from now on.' When John showed Stormy where he had in mind, visibility was poor, there was a strong icy wind, and the roads were becoming dangerous to be on. 'Gets like this from now on, locals can't work much, comes and goes quickly. Reckon this is what you were looking for?'

They had turned off the main road and driven up a rough dirt track. Stormy got out but couldn't see much except the middle of a high peaked wide rock with what looked like a split in the middle, the split opening going down so far, he couldn't see properly. 'How far down does it go?'

'No idea, never seen the bottom of it. If Clive, Jake or I were driving, we could find it blindfolded, as we have been tracking around these parts ever since we were kids. Can get a bit nasty though on the roads this time of year.'

Emmitt looks out his office window and sees Clones walking along the street with suitcases towards the Hospital Estate, he realized the situation in Huxley was becoming very serious and decided to see Sidney Carver with a plan that had been on his mind. When he arrived at their home, he was surprised to see the house being packed up.

Sidney greeted him warmly and explained. 'The wife and I have decided it's time to go before it's too late. We are going to take what we can fit into our rental, and the rest I'm going to lock into my garage, and hope will be alright till this madness is over.'

'Sidney, I want you to come and live with me,' said Emmitt, 'I have a large attic upstairs in my house if the situation worsens, live there no one will know you are in the attic. I will make it nice and comfortable for you all and get some extra supplies in each week so no one will notice. I've been hearing some threats made to the Clones going up to the hospital estate as they are walking along the street.'

'That's mighty kind of you Emmitt and I appreciate it, but to hide five people might be a bit of a crowd.'

'Well, the way things are going, the Hospital Shelter is going to be more crowded. There are only so many rooms in the shelter to accommodate all those that may want to go there. You know how I feel about Trace, would you let her come if things became dangerous, you must know how I feel about her. I love her, and want to marry her, and would do anything to protect her and help her family.'

Mazie Carver walked in with Trace, they had been in the kitchen and overheard the conversation. 'That's a wonderful offer Emmitt,' she said, 'but I think my husband is right, we are quite a tribe, but Trace is old enough to make up her own mind.'

The two of them sat down on the lounge in a corner so could be as private as possible. 'Well Emmitt, would have been nice to let me know how you feel and tell me first.'

'I know darling, I had intended to speak to you first, but these are not normal times.' He got down on one knee and said, 'I love you with all my heart Trace, please say you will marry me, and that you feel the same way. I want us to pick out a lovely ring together soon as possible, and I want you to come and live with me.'

Trace bent down and kissed him on the head, he got up and joined her on the lounge. 'I love you very much Emmitt, and want to marry you, but I'm not sure about living with you.' She put her hand over his mouth before he could speak, 'let me think about it.'

They got up, and she looked up into his face with love, and he could feel with his hands her body was trembling, he held her tight and kissed her longingly. Emmitt left the house with a promise to meet her at his office the next day to pick out an engagement ring from the jeweler who had a shop next to his in the town. Emmitt felt he was walking on air.

Fireman Chad Wiley saw the switchboard light up. He answered it, it was from an owner of a business in the High Street phoning from her shop, saying a bomb had been thrown through the window of the shop next to hers causing a fire, which was spreading quickly and was now coming into her business. He got her address and put it into his computer and knew straight away it was a Clone owned shop. 'Right, yes right. We will get there as soon as we can.' He was surprised to hear this, he knew there was a lot of people getting fed up with so many of them living in Huxley, but he didn't expect them to resort to this kind of hatred. He saw young Eddie who was on duty with him coming through the doorway from the kitchen with two mugs of coffee. *Lucky, he had been out of the way when the call came through,* he thought. All he had to do was act natural and wait for someone else to call which he knew would not be too long. He hoped by the time they arrived at the scene a great deal of damage would be done, enough even to prevent the shop owners from trading, but glad the lawyer chap was down the other end of the street as he was undergoing some important business for him, and he didn't want anything to interfere with that, as there wasn't any other lawyer in Huxley, and they were snowed in now and couldn't go elsewhere. The expected next call came through, he repeated what he had said before.

Eddie hands one mug of coffee to Chad. 'Who was that?'

'Woman who is working late in her shop in High Street, says someone threw a bomb into the shop next to hers and fire is spreading to her business. I got her address, and I know a Clone owns this business.'

'Oh well, let's finish our coffee first before we get into action. I don't like Clones.' He laughed, 'with a bit of luck there will be enough damage done so the shop owner is prevented from trading.'

'I'm glad the lawyer chap is further away down the street,' said Chad, 'as he is doing some important business for me at the moment. I don't want anything to interfere with that, there isn't any other lawyer in Huxley, and we are snowed in now and I can't go anywhere else.'

Emmitt could not believe what his eyes were seeing. He was standing just inside his office door. A large number of part Clones were walking up to the Hospital Shelter carrying what they could with their children. But what horrified him was the townspeople that were following the Clones on the footpath on the other side of the road. They were heckling them with '*good riddance, about time this problem is going to be solved.*' He saw that there were some women following who were crying. Two men came past looking at the scene not noticing he was nearby, one was saying to the other, 'it won't be long now, another couple of days and there should be most of them up there.' Emmitt wondered and worried about that overheard comment. It was time to act, he would have to get the Carver family into his home that night without fail, whatever was going to happen he would have them safely installed there. He had everything already prepared for Trace but needed to do more for the extra family members. He closed his office door and went up High Street slowly past the fire damaged shops on his left. At home he put more mattresses and other small furniture up into the attic, ready for the extra family. They would have to come, they would have to. Since the bombing of the shops near him in the town, he was on edge. That event had taken away the happy memory he had cherished of buying an engagement ring with Trace, but that would now have to wait, he felt deep down lives were at stake.

That night he had a struggle with Sidney and Mazie Carver to convince them they were in danger, even after hearing what he had overheard the two men saying outside his office they were hesitant. 'Surely Sidney after hearing what I heard those men say today, you must realize it's time to act. The bombing of the shops near me in Huxley has really put me on edge. You must realize the situation is now dangerous. I want you installed at my house so I will know you and your family will be safe.' At last Emmitt had an idea that might change the situation. 'Sidney if you just come now, tonight, with your family and everything is ok in a few days, say to the end of the week, then come back here. All I ask is that you come tonight, I have put extra mattresses and other things you will need, it will be quite comfortable for a few days. Surely, you cannot refuse to do that for the sake of your wife and children. I have blacked out the windows up there so no one will see a light at night.'

Sidney looked at his wife and children who had joined them. 'Alright Emmitt, perhaps it's the right decision, what do you think Mazie?'

'Well dear, I must admit I am feeling very nervous. Ever since Joan my neighbor, and a friend of hers just came into our house and started taking my jewelry and some of our things, saying we wouldn't be needing them, and warning us to leave Huxley I have been very nervous. I think we should all go, it will only be a few days and by that time, things might have settled down. We will come tomorrow night Emmitt. Let us all pack a case each with what we will need, also pack up some bed linen and I will clear all the food from the fridge to take with us. Just give us a day to organize ourselves.'

'It will take two trips to get you all and your luggage to my place tomorrow, we will go late at night. I will drive by the back streets away from the main streets so no one will see us.'

Sidney went with Emmitt to the front door. 'With all this trouble lately,' said Emmitt, 'I have become very concerned about the situation for Clones in Huxley. It is obvious that with so many here now things must change, and the best way to do this is to have a Clone on the Huxley Council. I have decided when the present situation has settled, I am going to start a voting campaign for a position on the Council at the next elections which are not far away. I was hoping you would support me, help me with setting things up. If you are agreeable, perhaps the family would be willing to help distribute flyers and so on.'

'I would certainly help Emmitt. You are right, it's the only way things will change, but as you said let's get over this difficult period first. Have you spoken to others?'

'I have, and not only in the Clone community, many other decent people in Huxley and even some living in the surrounding villages feel we are being unfairly treated and would vote for me. I honestly feel I would have a very good chance of success.'

'You are a good man Emmitt and people trust you, but I am worried about one thing.'

'What's that?'

'Your safety Emmitt. There are some very nasty people that have come into town, and they are dangerous. They won't want a part Clone on the Council, your life could be in danger.'

Emmitt collected all the Carver family and their luggage the next night and drove his crowded car around the back streets as far from the main roads as possible. By midnight, they were reasonably settled. He takes Trace by the hand and leads her away from the others. 'Trace I feel less anxious about you and your family now you are all here with me. I'm so sorry we didn't get the chance to go and buy your engagement ring, the jeweler has closed his shop as too frightened after the bombing and fires. Whoever did that, has robbed us of what was going to be a happy occasion. We will get a ring as soon as he opens again and happier times are back or come with me to Sydney when I visit my parents, and we can choose one there. I am looking forward to you meeting them.'

'I can wait Emmitt. I would rather get a ring when there is less worry. They kiss passionately. Trace pulls herself away reluctantly. 'I must go and help, everyone is on edge. Thank you for everything Emmitt, I love you so much.' He goes with her to the stairs and watches her go up and goes into his bedroom.

At last, at last, thought John Hislop, possessing the lawyer's home was behind all his hard work which was now going to happen as he planned it. As he parked his van outside Emmitt Benson's home, he Clive and Stormy started up the slight incline to the house.

Clive was nervous. 'Why couldn't we have waited dad, we should be with the others who are just about ready to start doing the dirty work getting rid of the scum. Why aren't we there as well?'

'Shut your mouth Clive, I have waited a long time for this moment. I want this lawyer's house more than anything I've ever wanted. I hate his guts so much it's killing me. I just want to have a look around. I won't be long, after we will go straight to the hospital and help our mates finish the job.'

Clive was looking around very nervously, 'how do you know he's not here dad?'

'Because I happened to see him driving up towards the Hospital Estate earlier in the evening. He would be up there with that girl he's been going out with. Makes you sick just thinking about it, more baby Clones on the way before long.' John Hislop walked around the home and tried all the doors and windows. 'All locked up, nice and tight. Don't want to break or smash anything. Let's get this job done, and I will come back with some tools tomorrow.'

On the way back along the lane they saw two figures walking along carrying a suitcase each, they had a torch so could see where they were going.

'Hello, hello said Stormy what have we here? Bet these two are going up to the hospital.' They followed the pair slowly, and then went past them, and saw two women, one young one, and one older.

'John, stop the truck, let's have some fun.'

Clive called him back, he was very nervous, his father got out and joined him. Stormy and John accosted the women, who started to run away, but the men caught up with them.

'Leave us alone,' the older woman said. 'We don't have any gold jewelry or money as my neighbor has taken everything. We are on our way to the Hospital Shelter.'

'Well, if you haven't got any jewelry, there's only one other thing my mate and I are interested in. Be nice.'

Cassie and Leanne Harris screamed and tried to get away, but the men were too strong for them, and they were forced to the ground. Cassie kept screaming so loud that John became angry and hit her so hard she became silent and dazed. After he raped her, he strangled her.

Stormy did the same to Leanne. They stood up pulled up their trousers and adjusted themselves. Clive heard the women screaming as they struggled with the men, but they were soon on the ground and Clive knew what was happening. He wanted to go home this was not fun. The two men started pulling the women by their hands to the back of the van. He heard the back doors open, and Stormy said, 'just as well we got the van all lined up, here are our first donations, and they threw the two bodies in. 'John we better go back and collect their suitcases and anything else, mustn't leave anything behind.'

Afterwards, John and Stormy were in a very good mood, talking and laughing all the way to the hospital. They parked under the trees surrounding the hospital further down a slope. John saw his son's ashen face and said, 'what's the matter with you Clive? You're as white as the snow. What do you care? They were only Clones for heaven's sake. Stay by the vans so you can help the others pile as many bodies inside as can fit as they are brought out to the trucks and vans.'

Stormy added, 'if any try to get away, go after them and hit them hard on the head, leave them where they are, and get back to the vans, they can be picked up last thing. The snow will cover any blood before morning.'

Dana was in her kitchen, she had prepared tea which was almost ready, it was now dark, and she hoped Scott would not be long. He had phoned earlier saying he would be late as a baby coming that was taking some time due to complications. She had already got the fire in the lounge firing up nicely, so it would be nice and warm by the time they sat down to eat. Dana was used to late meals, babies came at all times she had learnt to live with it. She heard her name called out, and looking out the window was surprised to see Scott running towards the house. He rushed inside gasping for breath, while locking the kitchen window and pulling the curtain across said, 'quick Dana' he propelled her into their lounge-room. 'We have been notified that a large mob of people are on their way up to the hospital and they are armed. They've cut the telephone wires, and we have lost all communication so I couldn't contact you. I haven't got long darling, so listen carefully as I have to get back to the hospital. I want you to lock yourself up in the house. You must stay in the lounge or bedroom and don't come out. Get all the outside screens down. I don't think this mob is in the least interested in you. It's the hospital and the Shelter and the Clones in it that they are angry about, so promise me,' he shook her by the shoulders, 'promise me, that you will not under any circumstances go outside for anything, even if someone bangs on the door. Do you understand?' She dumbly nodded. 'I must get back to the hospital as I have a woman almost ready to give birth, and she will need me. She is a Clone.'

She grabbed him by the arm, 'please don't leave me Scott,' she pleaded, 'I need you, and you know you are in danger too. Let Doctor Burgess look after your patient.'

'Well, that's the problem darling, Todd and most of the other staff couldn't get out of there fast enough as soon as they got the word that so many are coming, and all riled up.' Scott went quickly around the house locking all the windows and doors. He hesitated by the front door, looked back, blew her a kiss, and said, 'you know how much I love you. I wanted to see you and know you will be safe,' and was gone. She heard him lock the door with his key, and his footsteps running away.

Dana, looking out the large lounge window, saw a group of people climbing up the rise to the hospital, the outside front area was well lit. They appeared to be angry, brandishing pieces of wood, and she saw some carrying hunting rifles. They all had their faces covered dressed in ski suits. When they reached the hospital, they started banging on the main door, she could hear sounds of wood splintering, smashing, screams, chaos. She picked up her phone to call the police, but there was no response. She pulled across the thick curtains and lowered the outside security screens, did the same in all the rooms then went back and sat in Scott's favorite armchair, covered her ears with her hands and sobbed.

Joe Waverly inside the hospital knew his daughter's Clone lover was here somewhere, and he knew he had a perfect opportunity to get rid of the problem, at the same time help the others get rid of as many Clones as he could. He owed it to all the other parents in the area to not have to go through the torture he and his wife had these last weeks. No one would know who killed who, they were all dressed the same with hoods and gloves on. Couldn't be more perfect. There was little resistance, sheep to the slaughter. The staff remaining was locked into two rooms. He with the others went through all the rooms one by one. Dragging them out of the rooms, or patients out of their beds. Men, women, and children. As they were deposited by the trucks and vans, those there with no hesitation pulled them by arms and legs and threw them into the waiting vehicles. Joe Waverly couldn't see his particular Clone anywhere, everything was happening so fast as was arranged, he just had to hope someone else had done the job. He didn't dare ask if anyone had seen him, they didn't know who he was anyway. Feeling very hot he pulled his Balaclava off to wipe his face.

'Cover your face, you idiot,' John Hislop said angrily, 'no one must recognize any of us.'

Joe, John and Stormy with the others went through all the rooms of the hospital and the adjoining Shelter one by one, dragging out Clones hiding in rooms. There was little resistance. They were deposited down by the vans to be manhandled by those waiting to squeeze as many as possible into the vans. Some try to get away, they were chased and clubbed down on the spot and left.

Stormy was at John's van, pushing in Clones with Clive helping. Last one was a girl who was very quiet and resigned like most of them. 'Here you go Clive, brought you a nice little Clone to play with.

Help yourself when we get up there.' He closed the door and locks it, 'you're full up.'

Doctor Scott Benson had just delivered a beautiful baby boy unassisted. He laid him down on his mother's exhausted body, the cord still attached. He had the surgical tool in his hands to cut the cord when the double operating room doors were flung open, and two armed men came in coming straight for him. Scott stood in front of his patient and child trying to shield them but was struck on the head with the butt of a rifle, and half dazed was pulled out of the operating room and building. He caught a glimpse of the small mother clutching her child being lifted off the bed and forced to walk behind them, the cord still attached to the baby. Once outside he could hear all the screams and crying. He tried to wrench himself free to go to help his patient but was hit again and blacked out.

Stormy called out to the men with instructions, 'this is all that are in the hospital, just collect all those who tried to get way and are lying in the snow. Then we will go through those cabins on the estate, just in case not all went into the hospital. But remember, don't go near the two large homes adjoining the hospital grounds as they belong to those medical staff that are not Clones, they are doctors, people who run the place.' He added, 'you drivers bring the vans around the other side closer to the cabins, so we don't have so far to go.'

Time passed, and Dana had not moved. Scott had not come back to unlock their door. There were now voices only to be heard further away outside on the front areas of the hospital. Tentatively, she brought the lounge screen a short way up and kneeling on the floor looked out onto the grounds and saw dead bodies everywhere lying in the snow. Perhaps her husband, her friends, her patients. Bodies were being pulled along by their arms or legs, collected like trash to be disposed of. No remorse shown, she even heard a few laughs from men as they dragged the bodies down the slope, she couldn't see where they were going. She realized it was a well pre planned collective effort. No evidence was to be left for the country to find.

It only took about 90 minutes before Clive Hislop was on the road again, but it had seemed an eternity. The vans all went up the dirt track now covered by snow, waited their turn to dump their cargo. John and Stormy stood either side shooting any Clones that were still alive in the head and threw them down over the side of the mountain to make sure all was done properly, and all evidence thrown down with the dead. Each driver's clothes, shoes, masks and gloves also thrown down. John Hislop was enjoying himself playing games with some of the women by making out he was going to throw their child down before them alive holding them out over the side of the mountain in mid-air. When he threw one child down alive, Stormy quickly shot the distraught mother and threw her down, not knowing whether the child was now dead or still alive with all the bodies below.

John Hislop got all the men together before they left. 'Well done everyone, you all followed orders perfectly, take what you want from tomorrow as per our meeting last night. You all received your share of the loot collected leading up to tonight. Keep quiet, and we are all in the clear. The bodies will never be found they're too far down, but just to be on the safe side as extra precaution Stormy and I are going to chuck some soil down there when the weather a bit better before summer, followed by some local grass seeds that will soon take hold which will help to cover the spot.' As an afterthought he added, 'don't forget what I told you about checking inside your trucks, they were lined but wash them thoroughly.'

Stormy pulled Clive to one side. 'Well, how did it go, enjoy yourself? I don't remember you coming back with that Clone.'

Clive looking miserable, 'she just laid there. she didn't put up a fight or anything. I lost her.'

'You bloody what, how?'

'I went out the back of the van to clean myself up a bit and did a pee. When I turned around to get her, she was gone! I looked everywhere for her. It was so cold she couldn't have gone far but it became so foggy I couldn't see very well. Dad is going to kill me.'

'Bloody hell! I'll tell your father over a few drinks. She couldn't have gone far we will come back tomorrow and get her during the day. She will be frozen. We'll chuck her down with the others.'

Stormy brought out a bag he had stuffed under the front seat of John's van and said, 'Clive, John, let's have a little private party,' and pulled out some whiskey.

'Not here mate, the weather is coming up bad, visibility will be almost gone soon, we had better get closer to Huxley,' adding, 'Clive looks like he badly needs a drink.'

'I've had enough for one night dad, take me home before you start drinking.' His father looked at him with a worried look. 'Don't worry dad, I won't say anything.'

When they settled in a quiet spot not far from Huxley. 'My mates will settle down in the town' said Stormy, 'find an empty house to live in, they will keep order from now on. I wonder how many we got, I lost count, and I wonder how many are left in the town?'

'Don't worry,' said John, they will be traumatized and will get out of the area soon as they can. They won't say anything, they will be too afraid.' He was silently thinking for a moment. 'The town is ours. We have the Police, the Mayor and the Chief of the Fire Brigade under our control, what have we to be afraid of. No one will ever find the bodies.'

'John there is one problem that we are going to have to fix tomorrow. One of the Clones we took up there is missing.'

'What do you mean missing?'

'When Clive and I were packing up your van I pushed a young Clone girl in last before locking the door and told Clive when we got up the mountain and he had emptied your van, he could just park to one side and help himself before handing her over to be disposed of. Thought it would make a man of him, and it would be less likely he would say anything in the future about what we did if he was in the same position. He took me up on it and I saw him park the van to one side after he emptied it, but I didn't see him bring the girl back. When he finally showed up, he said when he had her, he went outside to pee and when he turned round, she was gone. He looked everywhere for her but couldn't find her.'

'I'll kill the fucking little bastard!!!!!'

'She couldn't have gone very far, half dressed in this freezing weather, we will find her body and put it down with the rest.'

'You stupid bastard!' John was furious. 'I worked the time out for this, and the weather is going to be that bad for the next three days, no detectives will be able to get up here in a helicopter which will give plenty of snow cover over every bit of evidence, and where the bodies are. How in the hell do you think we are going to find a body in the deep snow we are going to have? We may not be able to even get up there. As it is, no one will ever be able to find where we have thrown them, but if they find a body, the police will draw a circle around it and explore that area and might find where they are.' He was quiet thinking for a while. 'She would be frozen solid, but these days I think they have ways of getting samples of men's milk, they will find out she's been raped, which they could trace back to Clive, and if he's in police hands long enough we are done for. Looks like we have to get up there as soon as we can and find that Clones body.'

Next day word travelled very fast around the town and outer villages. Andrew Bishop was having a lie in as had been on night duty. His next-door neighbor came over before he left for work to tell him the news. Andrew couldn't believe what he was hearing. quickly dressing, not bothering to put his uniform on, he rushed into the police station to talk to Jerry and Brenton. Both said that everything was normal at the concert, and they had only just heard themselves when they got to the police station. Mayor Kingsley had phoned with the news, yet they didn't seem very concerned.

Andrew was appalled, 'what are we going to do?'

'I've already done the only thing we can do,' said Brenton. 'I have been on the phone to our superiors in Sydney and reported the matter. They told us to collect as much information as we can, and make enquiries for our report, but they can't get up here at present. Weather report says extreme weather for next few days so too dangerous to send a helicopter up with detectives. So, we will do the best we can until help arrives.'

'How many were killed do you know?' asked Andrew.

'Who said anything about anyone being killed? If you're thinking of those two women you were interested in, you had better go and look them up for yourself, and then go to the hospital, one of us will join you.'

Andrew quickly went out the door, Jerry called out after him, 'better get your uniform on before you do anything, this is not private, it's police business.'

Later Andrew was to remember his colleague's reactions, it was as though they had known about this beforehand, they didn't seem surprised, and he wondered why he had been asked to do night duty. He didn't want to believe it was because he would be out of the way. There had been no emergency calls during the night. All very strange.

Cassie and her mother were not at their house, but their neighbor Joan and some other women were, they were inside going through all their things and putting items into bags when he called. His heart almost stopped beating he knew the answer before he asked the question. 'Where are Cassie and Leanne Harris?'

'They went up to the hospital last night,' said one of the women. 'I saw them from my back kitchen window walking up the lane behind my house it was very late. They had a torch to see where they were going, so I saw them clearly.'

'Put all their things back, you are stealing,' said Andrew angrily.

'Why', said Joan, 'they won't be needing these things anymore and didn't have any relatives, Leanne told me so.'

Andrew couldn't speak, he left, he knew he had let these women down, his Cassie down, by not insisting they go to him. He didn't do enough.

It seemed as though the whole community was a tight-lipped whole, no one knew anything, no one heard of any plans to go to the hospital. He questioned one of the night nurses still there. 'I don't know anything we were all locked into a room. I didn't see anything.' Another nurse said. 'How could I see anything locked in a room. I did hear some yelling that's all. They were told to leave, and they left. Don't upset the patients, they were traumatized enough with staff disappearing last night and now police asking them questions.' All Andrew heard was the Clones were told to leave, and they must have planned something beforehand. When he said they couldn't leave because of the weather, they just looked away and repeated they knew nothing. A few where bold enough to say, 'good riddance.'

Talking to people in High Street was the same. 'You're the policeman, it's your job to find out. Leave me alone.' Some walked around him to avoid speaking to him.

Back at the police station Andrew spoke to Jerry. 'It's as though the community is a tight-lipped whole, no one knows anything, no one heard of any plans to go to the hospital. When I answered they couldn't leave because of the weather, they just looked away, repeating they knew nothing about what happened.'

'Go home Andrew, you have been working all day, and you were on night shift last night. You look exhausted. Go home, get something to eat, and get some sleep.'

'Not until I've finished making out my report,' said Andrew.

Brenton called on Andrew a couple of days later. 'We haven't seen you Andrew for a few days, so I thought I had better come and see how you are?'

'Well mate, you can see how I am. I'm watching TV.'

Brenton could see the news which was a discussion between a female journalist and a Doctor Ramsey, a University psychologist in Sydney. She had asked him, 'what makes one person want to kill another person or in this case possibly Clones?'

Doctor Ramsey continued. 'They are different, too many of them, fear, prehistoric fear of something you don't know, they would take their homes, overrun the nearby towns. Have to protect themselves. There are many reasons.'

Brenton could see Andrew was listening intently, unshaved, with a large bottle of beer in his hands, he was drunk and in a bad way. 'I'll put you down for sick leave mate until the end of the week. You need some time to get yourself together.' He didn't get any answer, so he left. Back at the station he said to Jerry. 'You should see him Jerry, he's a mess, hadn't shaved and empty beer bottles scattered around. Hope he pulls himself together before these detective chaps come here next week with a search party. God knows what he might say to them.'

'Doesn't matter anyway, we are covered, we were at the concert and didn't hear anything, plenty of witnesses saw us there. He was here by himself and didn't leave as on night duty. One person phoned earlier to speak to me, but was told I was not available, so, he was definitely here. We have nothing to worry about.'

'If he is the same, we will just say he was in love with one of the female Clones who left, and it's got to him,' said Brenton.

Wendy Coulter a prominent Journalist for Channel 20, who had set herself up with her crew in front of the Town Hall in Huxley, was having difficulty getting local people that passed by to talk to her, so far only a few were willing to get in front of the camera. She had been hoping for sensationalism, but the answers were boring. 'I don't know anything about any Clones being killed, it didn't happen,' or 'someone has just made up this story for news, no, I have no idea where they are, they were told to leave, and they did.' She did note however, which she made sure her viewers were made aware of, was that there was no concern or remorse shown as to what had happened to them. Perhaps nothing had happened to them?

One person only admitted they didn't like Clones, and said, 'glad they are gone, good riddance,' and walked away.

When four detectives came up to Huxley when the weather temporally improved, they received the same replies. A man named Stormy was arrested as was a known criminal with a violent history, and a couple of locals as well who had voiced how they hated the Clones, but they could not be detained permanently, as after limited searches no bodies were found. The detectives returned to Sydney, with a plan to organize a large search party soon as the snow depth was less, and the bad weather improved.

Andrew very drunk, slowly, walked out of his house, his arms hanging down by his sides, a beer bottle in one hand and his gun in the other. He went down the lane where he knew Cassie had walked with her mother to go to the hospital on that fateful night, he had been there before just wanting to be where she had walked. He was listlessly walking along and saw a small piece of colored material fluttering in the strong wind amongst a thorny bush. He threw the bottle away, walks carefully to where it was caught on a twig further back from the side of the lane. He recognized the material it was from her scarf that she wore the day of their picnic in the mountains. He carefully untangled it and pressed it to his lips, put his gun to his head and shot himself.

Part 3 – Clone Hospital Massacre

When left alone the raped girl grabbed the man's jacket lying on the floor of the van, slipped into her shoes and jumped out quietly, moving away from the urinating man and ran into the trees. She didn't know where she was going, just that she had to get away, otherwise she knew she would be killed, and she did not want to die. She heard the man coming through the trees looking for her. With closed eyes she stood still behind a large tree, and he did not see her in the van lights. Before everyone had left the scene, she was on the move knowing moving was her only hope of survival. She put the jacket on, but still felt very cold, it was snowing lightly. Stumbling down a hill, she came to a snow-covered narrow track and followed it. Walking, stumbling, she kept going knowing she was running out of energy. She stopped, she could smell smoke, no, she was imagining it, a trick of the mind, so continued, soon the smell became stronger. Smoke meant fire and warmth it forced her on. She fell tripping over a branch, struggling up she could see a light, was she dreaming. No, she stumbled towards a small cabin. There was an outbuilding near it, she entered and there were piles of wood in there, many large bags were in a pile, they were cold when she put them around her and collapsed exhausted, too afraid to see who might be in the hut.

Igor was sitting by his warm *izba* log fire with his dog Oskar, his companion of many years. Oskar pricked up his ears, raised his large body and walked towards the door, looking back at Igor and barked. Igor put his book down, goes to the door and takes his warm lambskin coat from the hook with the wool inside and the skin outside. Igor lit a lamp, picked up his hunting rifle, opens the door and slips out quietly closing the door behind. Both go to the side of the hut and listen. Oskar goes to a small shed nearby, and barks again. Igor goes inside holding his lamp up high, his rifle at the ready in his right hand. Oskar goes to the back of the wood pile, Igor follows. They see a young woman lying with sacks over her. She is almost frozen and appears near death. Slinging the rifle strap over his shoulder, he picks her up and carries her into the *izba*, Oskar following. Igor knows he might be too late, lays his sheepskin coat on top of the Russian stove, covers it with material and a pillow at one end, lays her on it, covers her feet with footcloths, motions Oskar to lay next to her and covers them both with two thick rugs. Putting some vodka in a cup, Igor tries to get the girl to drink. He persevered repeatedly but could only get her to swallow a small amount, he continued this night vigil, that night and the next night. He had given up hope, when she sputtered and coughed as he gave the girl more to drink. He had broth all ready and gave her some, after swallowing a few spoons of broth, she fell back exhausted and went to sleep.

As the days, weeks passed she got better and ate more. Igor asked her questions, but she never answered, it was as though she did not hear him. She had her arms around Oskar most of the day, and the dog did not leave her. Igor knew he would have to go soon to the village to get some more provisions to add to what he had preserved, otherwise he would be completely snowed in without the necessities to last the winter. The woman at the store would be waiting to get the old miners' wood toys he had whittled which were popular with the winter tourists. He needed to exchange them for flour, dried milk, sugar, tobacco and Vodka. He hoped he might get some news about the girl, who was gradually getting stronger but still frightened whenever he asked her what had happened to her, so he stopped asking. When in the village Igor always went to the Log Inn next to the Trading Post store for a few drinks and a meal before returning home. He hated it in the village, always had, but he might hear something there. At night he talked to the girl. He named her Zoloto, the Russian name for Gold. She listened intently, looking at him with her wide sad eyes. He told her how he had come to these mountains as a young man with his good friend Nikolai. They had grown-up together, they were *Muzhik's*, poor peasants, there was much trouble and fighting in Russia and Europe. They went to different countries, could only find a little work, food and much sadness. When they heard that gold was found in Australia, they decided to come and look for it in this far away land. They finally received a visa and worked on a ship which landed in Sydney, they gradually made their way to the mountains with hundreds of other men all hoping to make their fortunes. They found some gold, but not enough. Others heard of another place called Victoria, but Igor did not want to leave the mountains, as it reminded him of home, so Nikolai decided to stay with him. They built this *izba* which was like the log huts they had in Russia and they made a life there. It was a good life until Nikolai became ill, he died, and Igor buried him not far from the hut.

One day Igor taught Zoloto how to cook *pelmeni*. 'When I was young, my *babushka* taught me how to cook *pelmeni*. In Russia she used lamb, beef and sometimes pork for the filing of the little pillows, but I only have lamb. Before you arrived, I slaughtered my animals I buy every year. Then I cut up the meat, so I have food for the winter.' Igor showed her how to mince the meat, cut some onion and mixed it all up. He then put some flour, salt, and added eggs with a little warm water into a bowl, mixed it up then pulled pieces of it off and squeezed it over and over with his thick strong hands, singing a Russian folk song as he did so. Zoloto helped Igor with rolling out the rounds of pastry and filling the little pillows with some of the minced meat, sealing the sides to make a half-moon, then pulled the two edges together making small crowns. It was the first time the old man saw a spark in the young woman's eyes. She was interested in what he was doing. 'Zoloto my child, I want you to make some more *pelmeni* while I am gone. I must go into the village to get some supplies otherwise we will not have enough to make bread. I need to buy more flour, salt, and sugar. My tobacco is becoming very low and so is my Vodka which makes life more bearable for old Igor. I have enough small wood *babushkas* to exchange for the things I need. The lady who owns the Trading Store shop will be wondering why I have not arrived, as she sells a lot of my toys to the tourists who come to the mountains in the ski season.'

He showed her a wood box with a lid that was attached to the wall outside under the window. Lifted the lid and put all the *pelmeni* in smaller separate bags inside. That night he took one bag of the frozen dumplings out and put them in boiling salted water. He showed her the little dumplings floating to the top. 'That's how you know they are ready when they float to the top.' They sat down to eat, Igor put some of the bouillon they were cooked in around her portion, he put vinegar on his. He put beside them both a small cold glass of Vodka.

Early next morning Igor showed her how to make a simple damper. 'Zoloto, while I'm gone make some damper which is an Australian word for bread.'

He put three cups of flour in a bowl with a little salt and a small cup of water, mixed it up with his hand made it into a rounded ball, put in on the end of a long wood handled metal spatula and pushed it into the oven.

'Now keep your eyes on it, you don't want to burn it.'

When it was ready he sat down with her, pulled it apart and got out a tin of 'Honey Syrup' poured some over it. It was warm, sweet and delicious.

'It makes a good breakfast, or sometimes you can make tea to have with it while I'm away. There's also some roast dripping in the cupboard you can eat with it.'

Zoloto became very agitated when Igor packed his wooden toys into a bag, wound his footcloths around his feet and put on his *ushanka*, and his *valenki*. He ordered Oskar to stay with her, promising he would not be gone for more than a few days, and to do the cooking and cleaning work he had taught her while he was gone. He left with some misgivings.

In the town he did his usual business with the owner of the Trading Post store. In a small glass cabinet on the counter were some little boxes with pictures of chocolates on the front. He decided to buy a box of chocolates for Zoloto. The woman said nothing when he paid for them but remarked to her eldest son who helped her in the store, that it was strange that he wanted chocolate, as had never bought any before. At the Log Inn Igor had a few Vodkas and was feeling warm and pleased with his purchases of supplies and his present. There was a small television there high up on the wall. He could see a lot of people there with police, they were asking people did they know something, but they were all saying they knew nothing, that people had left from somewhere. Cloe the barmaid saw him looking at it and explained.

'Police are looking for a lot of Clones that have disappeared, but no one knows anything.'

'Cloe what is a Clone, what do they look like?' Igor asked.

'Well, I've never actually seen one myself except on the TV. They are very slim, have pale grey rings around their eyes, and don't smile. Lots of them had gone to live in Huxley, lots of tourists around that area go to ski in the snow season. Seems they were not wanted there, locals don't like strangers living in their towns anywhere in these mountains, and they were taking jobs away from the local residents.'

'Why was there so many in this place Huxley?'

'Because the train comes up from Sydney there. Huxley is the terminus. No trains now of course, they are pretty much snow bound now.'

On the way home, Igor thought about the news he had seen and heard. Zoloto didn't look like other women in the village, she was very slim and had pale grey rings around her eyes.

In the Sydney Police Headquarters, Chief Inspector Little was with Investigators Josie Palmer and Alden Miller who were getting briefed before leaving for their new job in Huxley.

'Josie, I want you to go undercover, preferably at the local hotel, best place to hear anything that might help Alden who is going to be going in there for meals, which will enable you to pass on any information easily in your line of work without raising any suspicion. He will have a room there.'

'Chief, there must be someone who has said or seen something as to where the Clones are. So many people just don't disappear?'

'Well, Alden, that's just what's happened. No one is saying anything. Those that have gone to Huxley to investigate before you were confronted with ignorance, and complete indifference, saying they left. The train can't get up there through the tunnel this time of year, and the place is pretty much snowed in. Tourist buses go up by a safer back road for the ski season. This year has been more snow than usual, that's why I'm sending you up earlier than arranged because weather not too good next week.'

'How do I know if I can get a job at the hotel?' said Josie.

'Josie, this is the ski season. Lot of skiing and tourists. The hotel is open almost around the clock, you shouldn't have much trouble.'

'What about the local police, will they know I'm there?'

'No, and they must not know Josie, they will only know about Alden.'

'Chief, who are the police there? They must be a useless lot,' said Alden.

'There are two senior officers, Brenton Ridge and Jerry Nelson. There was a third, a younger police officer, name of Andrew Bishop, who had only been up there a few months. Regrettably he shot himself.'

'Why?' asked Josie.

'The two senior officers stated he was in love with a young part Clone, and when she disappeared, he went to pieces, got drunk and shot himself. The officers said he blamed himself. Trouble had been brewing for some time between the locals and the Clones. He apparently had tried to get them to leave, but they refused, he felt he should have done more. You will be issued with guns, find a good place to hide them. You might need them.'

'Why? Sounds like an ordinary missing persons' case.'

'There is a criminal element in the town Alden. A small group have the town in their grip. The main two of this group is a man called Stormy, nasty piece of work, also a chap called John Hislop a known Clone hater, they and some of their mates are living in the homes that the missing Clones owned. Be on your guard, something not right there at all.'

'How long will we be there?'

'At least a week or two Josie. Depends, what progress you both make. Neither be a hero. Good luck. Our helicopter leaves to take you up to Huxley in another two hours.'

He looks after them with a thoughtful, worried look.

Inspector Alden Miller walked into the Huxley hospital unannounced, taking staff by surprise, the Hospital Principal phoned the Mayor to let him know. Inspector Alden Miller always liked to take people off guard, he got answers that way. A senior nurse immediately followed him showing him around. 'Where are the Clones, and where are their separate rooms?' Opening up his notebook, as walking along the corridors. Totally unprepared for this question, the nurse somewhat flustered, led him to the back of the hospital pointing to the closed doors of several rooms. Inspector Miller looks inside all the rooms.

'Where are the Clone patients?'

'There aren't any here at present.' Her answer was abrupt and quick.

'Nurse, how many where here before the Clones disappeared?'

'I think you had better talk to the Hospital Principal.'

'You must know, you are the senior nurse here.'

She stammers. 'I was not here on night duty, I only do day shifts.'

'Really! Do you like Clones nurse?'

'That's none of your business, and I'm sick of being asked such questions'.

'Really! You must have heard something, tell me. Tell me now?'

The nurse walking away. 'I wasn't here, I don't know anything, speak to the night nurse.'

A man walks up to Alden and introduces himself. 'I am the Hospital Principal, please come to my office and I will answer any questions.'

Seated in the Principal's office, he is politely asked if he would like some tea. Inspector Miller would love some, but he refuses the offer of refreshments. Inspector Miller dives in without pleasantries.

'What happened the night Clones disappeared from your hospital?'

The Principal's story was what Miller was expecting and written in his file.

'In other words Principal, no one knows anything, staff were locked up in two rooms and didn't see anything. Clones had been asked to leave, and you say they did. It was very cold, and weather bureau said snowing so where do you think they went? Aren't you curious?'

'Of course.' He was very confident. 'I am sure it had all been planned well ahead of that night. There had been a lot of attacks on Clones Inspector, they were feeling afraid. Too many of them coming here this last summer, it was causing loss of work for the locals. They are different to us. Mountain people don't take too kindly to any changes to their way of life.'

'I see. Principal, do you like Clones?'

The Principal was irritated by the question.

'I do my best to look after this hospital and all those that are in it, regardless of their origin, color or beliefs. That is all, so we have finished I think, and I must get on with my duties.'

When outside the hospital Alden looks around the grounds, he sees one or two homes adjacent to the hospital, he goes up to closest one and knocks on the door. A woman opens the door and talks through the security screen.

'Yes?'

'My name is Chief Inspector Miller. I have come from Sydney to find out what happened here, and where the Clones are that have disappeared.'

'You had better come in. My name is Doctor Dana Bentlee. I was just going to make some tea would you like some?'

Gratefully, 'yes, I would, I have been busy today and not had a chance to stop for anything.'

Dana brings tea and biscuits in on a tray. She looks tired and ill. Miller gets up and takes the tray from her.

'You will have to excuse me Inspector Miller, I will tell you what happened as much as I know, but so far no one is interested in listening to me, and the Hospital Principal is telling everyone that I am acting as though I am mentally ill, because my husband and I worked here at the hospital. My husband was a part Clone and has been killed, and no one believes me.'

Gratefully drinking his tea. 'I really needed this. I want you to know that I am very interested, that is why I am here. I want you to take your time, tell me in your own words whatever you saw or heard the night the Clones disappeared.'

'I am a doctor here at the hospital, and also my husband Doctor Scott Bentlee, who was a part Clone. On the night you are asking about he had phoned me earlier in the evening, telling me he would be late as was attending a difficult birth. This was not unusual I am used to it. Later in the evening I was in the kitchen when I heard him calling out to me, I went to the window, this one here in the lounge as it over- looks the lawn area in front of our house and the hospital. He was running to our house, came in almost breathless, telling me the telephone wires had been cut and his phone was not working. He said that the hospital had received a message before they lost communications to say an armed mob was coming to the hospital, and they looked dangerous. Scott quickly came to tell me this, telling me not to open the door to anyone under any circumstances, and to close our security screens. He left because the woman he was attending was about to give birth, she was a Clone, and the other obstetrician and many of the staff were afraid and had left the hospital in a hurry to get out before the mob arrived, and he would not leave her.' She became very upset. 'I was afraid, also for him. I begged him to stay, but he kissed me, said he loved me and left. I never saw him again.'

He tried to steady her so he could get as much information as possible. 'Would you mind Doctor Bentlee if I had another cup of tea and another biscuit?'

Dana pulling herself together, poured another cup of tea and held out the plate of biscuits.

'What happened then, did you see or hear anything?'

'I immediately went from room to room closing the security screens, then came back to the lounge and looked out towards the front of the hospital which is well lit. I saw a large number of people all dressed the same, they were all in white ski suits walking up towards the hospital front entrance, all had weapons, baseball bats and some had hunting rifles. I quickly closed the blinds, and sat in the lounge unable to move, as I heard glass shattering, terrible screams, and yelling. It was a nightmare.'

'Did this go on for some time?'

'I lost all sense of time, it seemed a long time. Eventually it became quieter, so, I got up raised the outside security screen up just a short distance, knelt on the floor and looked out.' She hesitated, looking miserable.

'What did you see, Doctor Bentlee?'

'I saw bodies on the snow. They were being pulled by their arms or legs towards the edge of the grounds down the rise so couldn't see where they were taken. I heard some of the men laugh as they were dragging the bodies along. There was no remorse.'

Inspector Miller looked at her in sheer astonishment. 'I can't believe it. You are saying that the Clones from the hospital were massacred!'

'My dear husband was murdered Inspector Miller, and all the Clones in the hospital, as well as all those that came to the Hospital Shelter, which was at the back of the hospital thinking they would be safe there.'

Miller was visibly moved, he had not expected this.

'Do you believe me? I was taken away by some horrible men whenever anyone came asking questions at the hospital. Detectives from Sydney were convinced that I was a mental case and not worth speaking to.' She asked suddenly. 'Why did you come to my house?'

'For the simple reason the local police were notified I would be coming, but I came earlier and straight to the hospital to get people off guard. I just saw your home close by and just doing a routine door knock.' He was silently frowning taking in what he had just heard. 'I strongly feel you are in danger doctor, you did not see the actual murders, but you are a witness to seeing bodies on the snow, and you saw the mob approaching the hospital with weapons. I'll have to get you out of here and in a safe place.'

Dana was overwhelmed. 'You believe me?'

'I do indeed believe you Doctor Bentlee.'

'Then I had better tell you the rest of my story. I was only brought back here yesterday. The Hospital Principal came to see me and told me they need this house for the replacement obstetrician for my husband Scott's position at the hospital, for him and his family. He knows this house belongs to me, we built this house, and we were two of the founding members who invested years ago to build this medical complex in Huxley. He said I'll have to move, that they will put me in a very nice apartment more suitable for one person.'

'You have the papers to prove you are the owner Doctor Bentlee?'

'Yes, that's why I didn't make a fuss yesterday. I wanted time to collect all my legal documents for the land, home and plans of the hospital. I phoned our lawyer here in Huxley on my second mobile, his name is Emmitt Benson. He is the only lawyer here. I phoned him, told him what had happened. He thinks I have nothing to worry about and he wants to come and see me but unfortunately has a pressing situation to deal with himself at his own home. Emmitt is a half Clone and so is his fiancé, he admitted she and her family are living in his attic. It seems that there has been a man hanging around outside who wants to take over the property and is now trying to get into his house. He doesn't realize there is a family in hiding there and thinks Emmitt is alone. That person had not expected he would still be there after that terrible night. They are prisoners, he cannot leave the family alone.'

'Do you know the name of this stalker?'

‘Yes, I do, he is a Clone hater who has been stirring up the locals by the name of John Hislop, he and his mate Stormy have brought criminals into the town, they are taking control everywhere.’

Alden was very thoughtful. ‘Now there’s a name I have heard not long ago. Doctor, I am going to make one call to Sydney. Get your things together, travel light, and make sure you have any important documents relating to this house and complex, your husband’s will, and yours, be sure to bring all your jewelry, and money.’ And as an afterthought, ‘Oh, and you had better give me the phone number and address of your lawyer.’

That evening Inspector Miller comes into the dining room at the Huxley Hotel are sits down at one of the tables. Josie on the look-out for him, goes towards him with a menu. ‘Can I get you something to drink?’

‘Yes, bring me a glass of local white wine thanks. When you bring my wine, I’ll order. Charge the drink and food to my room 609, name of Miller.’

Josie comes back with a glass of white wine. Whispers, ‘anything?’ She has pad and pencil in hand, looking with interest at the menu he is holding up.

'Got a reliable witness today, had to act quickly and get the boss to send a helicopter up. I have just put her on it. We are dealing with mass murder, be very careful. What about you, you obviously got a job ok?'

Other diners start walking in. 'No trouble at all. I've nothing so far. I'm in room 305 downstairs where staff stay.' Louder, 'as you are looking for fish, I suggest the barramundi, or perhaps you prefer garfish.'

'The barramundi is fine, thank you.' Alden hands her back the menu. Alden enjoys his meal, but not the constant stares of other diners, especially those at the bar that are very hostile.

John Hislop was talking to Stormy at the bar drinking. 'That's him over there, got word he was here early, has made a nuisance of himself already at the hospital. Still lightly snowing but we are going to have to deal with that unfinished business, we can't wait.'

Stormy is very confident. 'Long as we can get up there, shouldn't take long.'

'You got no bloody idea. The body is most probably covered under snow, unless she went under some tree roots for cover or in a small cave. If we can't find her, we are just going to have to wait for the snow to thaw, hopefully he might be gone by then. In any case we have to find the body and get rid of it, as eventually when the weather gets warmer there will definitely be a search party up here looking round the surrounding area.'

Josie hears some of this conversation as close by. Something about a body, but she didn't hear enough for it to make any sense.

Stormy calls her over. 'Hey, gorgeous, you're a new face here. Get me another beer.' Stormy looks Josie over as she gets him another beer. 'I like the look of this one John, definitely my type. When we get our little job done, I'm going to chat her up.'

At the Huxley Police Station, police officer Brenton Ridge is talking on the phone as police officer Jerry Nelson arrives for work, he puts the phone down. 'That was the Mayor telling me that the Senior Inspector we were expecting is already here in Huxley and already making a nuisance of himself.'

Jerry looked surprised. 'Thought he was not due to get here until next week sometime. What's he been up to?'

'He went straight up to the hospital, tried to get information from some of the staff, and the Hospital Principal. Took them off guard. He's a smart one, not like those others they sent up.'

He's got some cheek,' said Jerry. He should have come to see us first. We are going to have to pay him a visit and show him some manners.'

'We'll do nothing of the kind Jerry, he'll be in to see us when he's good and ready. This one's dangerous, we will just have to see what he finds out.'

The phone rings, Brenton picks up and listens. Shouts into the phone. 'What, he did what! Why did you let her go back there anyway? I don't care if he wasn't expected till next week. You fool!' He slams the phone down.

Jerry is looking worried. 'What happened?'

'Doctor Bentlee was allowed to go home yesterday to pack a few of her things. The Principal had arranged that she was going to be shifted this morning to a unit with security, in one of the smaller villages where she couldn't be found. The Principal was going to get any papers or documents pertaining to her claim of owning her home and investing in the Hospital Complex because he wants her nice house as it's so near to his work. She's gone, and there are no legal documents left in her safe, which was left wide open. He thinks the Inspector must have gone there after he left the hospital. He's a hell of a smart one.'

'But where could he take her? We'll have to find her. I don't like this Brenton. I'm getting worried.'

'Jerry, just remember we weren't on duty that night. We were at a very loud concert. We didn't hear anything, and we don't know anything. Don't tell this Investigator anything else! Keep your mouth shut.'

Daniel was surprised when he saw Emmitt's number flashing on his phone. 'Anything wrong with the job I did for you Emmitt?'

'No Daniel, you did great work as always, that's why I know I can rely on you. I need you to do something for me straight away.'

'How can I help?'

'I'm going to have to trust you and confide in you Daniel. Before that terrible night our people disappeared, I have had a man hanging around my house, and now he is trying to get into my home. He was very surprised when he found out I was still here, and I didn't go up to the Hospital Shelter. He obviously thought he could just walk in and take over, but what he doesn't know Daniel is that I was so worried about my fiancé and her family that I brought them here the very night so many of the Clone community disappeared. I'm convinced they have been killed.

I cannot leave them alone and go anywhere, so I want you to erect a high fence around the property to keep people out, strong, but you can see through it to see who is out there if any dangerous people stalking the house. I want this started tonight when dark and you will need help. I will come out of the house and leave Sidney Carver my fiance's father, and her brother inside both with a gun for cover'.

'Both of my parents and I are in a secure hiding place which they prepared years ago when they first came here. No one knows they are here, as mother was warned by our neighbor who is a councilor to go to the Hospital Shelter, she most probably thinks that's where my parents went. I could ask my father if he would come with me.'

'If H200 could come with you that would be safer as that would be four men here. I will pay for any materials you have to buy.'

'Leave it with me Emmitt, I will speak to my father and let you know. I need to give this some thought.'

H200 who was sitting close by, was thoughtful. 'You didn't tell Emmitt I was here with you?'

'No dad, I didn't want to commit to anything without us thinking about it first, and we have to think about mum, she would be too frightened to stay here on her own.'

'You know as well as I do that trying to put up a fence at night would be a waste of time, it would get ripped up most probably the next day. We have to be cleverer than that.'

'Yes dad, this is where my little hobby will come in handy. I have already set up a nice surprise for anyone who should try and get in here, though very unlikely they would find us.'

'Daniel, we can't stay in here forever, and Emmitt can't either, as eventually we will need supplies, want to leave Huxley, or might need medical attention.' H200 looked at his son, 'your mother and I will never leave here. The authorities will bring Investigators here when the tunnel is clear and the trains are running again after the winter snow has melted. I'm sure they will get law and order back into Huxley when they find out who was responsible for the deaths of so many of our friends. I have to believe in the law, I have to.'

'Dad they will find out what happened, but it's a waiting game. In the meantime we have to help Emmitt, and those who are in his care.'

'What are you going to do Daniel? I will help in any way I can.'

'I'm going to give those criminals the fright of their lives.'

John Hislop and Stormy were up in the mountains, they were exhausted and totally fed up with looking for the girl who had escaped, and with each other. John hit Stormy on the back, hard, sending Stormy to the ground, he was in a real temper. 'This is all your fault you bastard, if you hadn't told Clive to have that girl, he would never have thought of it himself.'

'Not my fault she ran away. Clones are usually very submissive, unusual for her to run away like that.'

'She could be anywhere,' said John, 'if the Police search party find her they might find the others, they are frozen now but will be decomposing.'

Stormy got up and was dusting the snow off when John went for him and caught him off guard, hitting him so hard he went down again. He didn't like the look in John's eyes as he was coming towards him again. 'Take it easy mate, we could both do with a decent meal and a smoke. You know your way around these parts, where's the nearest place to get a beer?'

John stopped. The murderous look went out of his eyes. 'Come to think of it, there's an old mining town not that far from here, there's a store there called the 'Trading Post', sells all sorts of stuff, we can get smokes there and there's a little Log Inn alongside the shop where you can get a meal and buy booze.'

Inside the Trading Post, the two men bought cigarettes. Stormy liked the look of the little boxes of chocolates and decided to buy a box for Josie. John went outside to have a smoke.

The owner remarked, 'I haven't had many sales for these lovely chocolates, but now have had two men buy a box within a day of each other.'

Stormy looked interested, 'these are for a very nice lady I want to impress.' 'Well old Igor certainly wouldn't want to impress a lady at his old age, but I thought it strange as he has never bought sweets before, and he has been coming here for years before he gets snowed in his log cabin up in the high mountains.'

'Must be a hard life for an old person up in the mountains. Is he all alone?'

'He and a mate were up in the hills prospecting for gold years ago. They stayed on when everyone else went. His friend died. He is all alone now, but he knows how to look after himself, a real hermit. But when I didn't see him this year, thought I might have to get my son to go up there after the winter and see if he was ok, as perhaps he might have had an accident or died.'

'It would be interesting to see the old gold mines how do you get there?'

'You have left it too late Igor will only just make it home. But my son could be your guide in the summer if you want to hire him.'

'Might do that, thank you.'

John was waiting outside, he was annoyed, 'why do you want to buy chocolates for a bar maid you stupid bastard.'

'I think she's worth it, she's not like the others. I've taken a serious liking to her. Giving her these might put me in a good light. Might even ask her out for a date and get to know her. I'll take it real slow with this one.'

'You're a bleeding idiot. Why should you get what you want, and I can't get my house?' He was jealous.' He looked nasty again, 'wait till she finds out you're a rapist and a murderer?'

Stormy lit a cigarette and turned around slowly, 'you thinkin' of telling her John?' he said very quietly.

'Just want that lawyer's house and car,' he answered sullenly.

'Let's go eat, I'm starved and need a beer,' said Stormy.

Sitting in the Log Inn Stormy eating a hot meal kept looking at John's face, and thought he had the look of insanity in his eyes. He was very thoughtful for the rest of their meal. He realized he would have to help John get his house, as he had definitely been threatened. John didn't seem to be worried that if he dobbed Stormy in, he would be convicting himself and Stormy's mates as well. This meant he was dangerous and would have to be got rid of if he got worse. He would try to get him the rewards he thought he was due to see if this would calm him down and bring him back to reason. This person was not the John he knew, this whole business had changed him.

Stormy brought John a beer and lent over the table in a confidential manner saying. 'I will get one of the lads to come with me tomorrow and see just what this lawyer's movements are. He has to go out sometime. I will think of the best way to get rid of him.' He thought for a minute, 'what happened to the girlfriend and her family?'

John suddenly became alive. He sat up straight. 'Bloody hell, forgot all about them, I didn't see them go over the side of the mountain and haven't seen them since that night.'

'Interesting. So where are they?'

'Bloody hell, he has parked them somewhere, he will try to go see them, most probably at night,' said John getting excited.

'Or, or',.... Stormy said thoughtfully, 'has them hiding in his house. If that's the case, all we have to do is get the girl, keep her hostage until he gets out of there. He's a lawyer, force him to sign the house and car over to you, so you have all the property - problem solved,' he felt exalted. He kept to himself the news he felt sure he knew where the escaped girl was, she wasn't going anywhere, the lady at the shop said the mining area was now completely inaccessible for the rest of the snow season, so he had time to get this other matter fixed first. He would need John's local knowledge and expertise to go into the mountains to find her when the time came, but he wanted to see if John became less volatile and calmer, otherwise there might be two reasons to go out into the mountains – just the two of them. He wasn't going to let anyone know what he suspected. He wasn't going to take any chances.

Inspector Miller was contemplating his next move. He knew he should be paying a formal visit to the

Huxley Police Station but was concerned about Emmitt Benson the local lawyer and for the family he was hiding in his home. He felt he couldn't wait, so put in a call to his boss Chief Inspector Little in the middle of the night with an urgent request. 'Sorry to wake you up Chief, but there is a situation developing here that is serious. How is Doctor Bentlee?' He listened. 'That's good, she is safe, but it's going to take a long time for her to come to terms with that terrible night, and what happened to her husband.'

'She has given us a complete report of what she saw, heard and experienced, which is a very good start Alden, but we need more. If only there was a witness who actually saw the killings, who knows who was responsible and not afraid to be a witness. The Clones that are left in the town are locked in fear of their lives, and it certainly appears from what we now know that the police and the hospital principal are involved in a huge cover up, and these are not all I should expect. You must be very careful.'

'I need backup, you heard the story concerning Emmitt Benson the local lawyer from Doctor Bentlee. I am going to see him early in the morning, but there is not a lot I can do on my own. Also, I'm worried about Josie. One of the main players Stormy, who you know, is making moves on her, which she is avoiding for now, but he is not a person to take no for an answer for long. I'm going to try and get local help, Emmitt should know men who are reliable. I will get back to you soon as I have news. This is a worse case than I ever could have imagined.'

'Unfortunately flying is now out of the question, it was fortunate Doctor Bentlee managed to get here. There is a major mountain road that runs up into the mountains. I have already made plans to get some police up there as soon as possible, but it will take time for them to get up there by road under difficult conditions, but help is coming Alden.'

This was good news to Alden, but he still had a sleepless night, so got up early went down to have coffee and a light breakfast, phoned Emmitt he was coming to see him and made his way to his house. Arriving at his home, the door was opened for him as he walked up the steps. 'Just as well you phoned Alden, I have turned off the electricity around the front door and ground floor windows. Daniel, a friend of mine and I were up most of the night setting it up. Anyone trying to get in is in for a nasty shock.'

'Very resourceful Emmitt. Can we go somewhere for a quiet talk?'

Emmitt led the way into his lounge. 'The family aren't up yet so we can have privacy here, except for Mazie Carver and Trace preparing meals in the kitchen during the day, they are living upstairs. I'm very pleased you contacted me, and very grateful that you acted so quickly getting Dana away to safety. I was naturally worried about her, but couldn't leave, as there has been this Clone stalker John Hislop hanging about the house, and he has tried to break in. He didn't know I was here the day after the massacre, obviously thought I was killed so came with tools and was preparing to break in. Got a terrible shock when he had my rifle pointed at him. Since then, he has been roaming around sometimes with a few of his cronies, hoping I would go out. Can't stay cooped up here forever. The locals don't have much to occupy them at this time of year unless they work at the ski resorts, so he has nothing much to do. I'm a prisoner here at present, and I want to get out to see as many of the Huxley residents as possible because I will be running for a place on the Huxley Council as there is an election coming up soon.'

'You don't want to leave Huxley Emmitt, soon as the roads and tunnel open again?'

'No, I had a good life here before thugs came into the town. My fiancé and I want to stay here, and so does her family. Where would they go, it would be the same again elsewhere? Getting on the council is the only way there will be any change for Clones, also there are a lot of decent people living here who are sick of the way things have been. We have an inept Police presence, greedy Mayor, and even the Fire Chief didn't act quickly enough when a Molotov cocktail was thrown into a business in the High Street. It was owned by a Clone, and she still hasn't been able to open. I suspect there is some bribery involved by these criminals that moved into our town by a person name Stormy, he and his mate John Hislop seem to be the ringleaders in all this trouble.'

'How could this happen Emmitt, how does a few bad men come to a town, convince the majority of the community that it was alright to condone murder? This was killing helpless, unresisting people in cold blood.'

'John Hislop had at least one meeting I know of getting everyone stirred up. People up here have been cut off for a long time, don't take kindly to people that are different, that are taking away work and undercutting wages. Worse still, they don't like their children fraternizing with the young part Clones.' He went on, 'lot of greed involved, they are told if they get rid of the Clones they can have their property, so many of them went about stealing property and pushing people out of their homes. Neighbors went into neighbor's homes, stealing their jewelry even from some while they were out in the streets. The authorities made no attempt to help keep law and order.'

'Well Emmitt, I'm the law, but only one person. At least Sydney H.O, knows now what has happened, but those that have investigated before me came up against a blank wall, no one knows anything, no one saw anything. Same at the hospital. I have to find a witness, preferably more than one who is willing to testify, someone who saw the massacre, and people come forward who have had their property stolen.'

Emmitt sighed. 'The Clones left are too frightened, all are very vulnerable, most will be gone when the tunnel is open again. I have to convince them that things are going to be different, and if they vote for me their lives will improve.'

'There is help on its way Emmitt,' said Inspector Miller, 'but unfortunately the extra police are having to come the long way by the main mountain road, but they will be here soon. This is only part of the trouble. We have to find out where the Clones are. They were murdered, we have to find the bodies.'

'Yes,' said Emmitt, 'with the police here we can get rid of these criminals, we can rebuild what's left of our lives and rebuild confidence in our town. We need to find where they are, if we can't at least we can put up a memorial to honor the dead with all their names on it, this must never happen again.'

'We still will need witnesses, otherwise the culprits can't be arrested and brought to justice. Are you able to get any other men to help you if these thugs try to get you out before the law reinforcements get here?'

'I have my fiancés father here, and another older son, also Daniel, who is hiding with his parents in a safe hiding place. He rigged my place up last night, has done the same where they are living.' He thought for a minute. 'Inspector you might need to come here as well, things could turn really nasty, your life could be in danger.'

'Thank you Emmitt, I can take care of myself. Please call me if you need me. I will tell you a strict confidence that there is another investigator here in Huxley, a woman, she works undercover at the hotel hoping to pick up some useful information. Unfortunately, this Stormy chap is taking more than a light interest in her. She is trained for this sort of thing, and so keeping him at bay, but he is becoming more insistent.'

'She is welcome to come here if her situation becomes unpleasant, we must stick together, it's the way we can survive. If she comes, see if she can bring some food away from the kitchen. We will be getting a bit low on supplies with more here.'

Inspector Miller nodded, 'very well.' He got up. 'Right now, I have to pay a visit to the local police who I'm sure are seething as I haven't called into see them as yet. I deliberately came early to get people off-guard.'

Stormy went into the Huxley Hotel to catch up with John, Clive, Jake and Ed. He sat down with a beer, and as John still hadn't arrived asked where he was. 'He's at that lawyer's house again,' said Clive, 'can't keep away from it. He tried to get in again through a window last night, and received an electric shock, gave him a terrible burn and the pain has made him even more crazy. I'm afraid he will do something stupid, especially now he knows the lawyer's fiancé and her family have been hiding there.'

'That's what I wanted to talk to you about, John has been acting very strange, gets a nasty look in his eyes.'

'I know,' said Clive, I went down to our shed this week and he was making all these Molotov Cocktails, lot of them all on the bench. I asked what they were for, and he said it was about time we threw a few more into Clone businesses of those that are still here. I told him that would only cause more trouble, and we could get found out.'

'Things have been going ok since that night everyone has kept their mouth shut. The Clones left in town are getting ready to leave when they can. We have all just taken what we wanted, things have never been so good. He is going to ruin everything the idiot.' Stormy was worried. 'He is losing his mind you can tell by looking at him.'

'It's because he hates the Clones so much, not getting the house he wanted is sending him crazy. If he could have just got the lawyer's property, he would have been ok,' said Ed.

'I made a plan to grab the lawyers' fiancé when we found out where she was, as a hostage, then we could force the lawyer to sign over all his property to John. I have had a couple of my mates keeping an eye on the place now we know where the family is, but they haven't set foot outside. Must have food supplies to last a few weeks, but they will have to run out sooner or later. Don't worry,' said Stormy, 'we will starve them out. 'Stormy got up, 'got to go, got a date with a very special lady.'

They all looked at each other in surprise. They could see him talking to the new girl behind the bar. They saw her get her things and they both went over to a table, and he was buying her a fancy drink. John Hislop came in at this moment, and they didn't like the look on his face as he was looking over at them. He said, 'you rotten bloody bitch. I'll get you!'

Inspector Miller didn't expect to get a warm reception as he entered the Huxley Police Station. He didn't know quite what to expect, and he didn't care. Protocol would have been considered if he had expected to get co-operation or indeed genuine interest, but because he had read the previous reports of his colleagues who had preceded him, he knew he wouldn't get any further in this case as they were like trained Cockatoos constantly repeating the same comments over and over again. In fact, Inspector Miller suspected there was a master puppeteer over their heads with strings attached to their hands and bodies controlling their every move.

Policemen Jerry and Brenton were repeating the usual routine without being asked, so Inspector Miller rudely interrupted them and asked, 'where do you think the bodies are?'

Jerry flustered. 'We just told you, they just left, it had been planned long before the night.'

'Really', was his sarcastic reply. 'They developed wings did they and flew away?'

'Course not.'

'Then stop telling me fairy tales, you know, and I know, that in the weather that night they had no way of getting out of Huxley. So, where are the bodies?'

Brenton stepped forward alongside Jerry. 'Who said anything about bodies? We don't know anything about the Clones being killed.'

Inspector Miller ignored him. 'What happened to your colleague police officer, Andrew Bishop, why did he shoot himself? He was a young man, only been here a short time, why weren't you looking after him?'

'You have no bloody right to speak to us like that Inspector.' Brenton was angry. 'It's all in the report we sent to Sydney, he was in love with a part Clone. We warned him about getting involved with this Clone and her mother, but he wouldn't listen. He tried to make them leave but they stayed. After that night he couldn't find them, got drunk, and shot himself. Must have felt guilty that he didn't do more to protect them.'

'Where did he shoot himself?'

Jerry was becoming nervous. 'In a lane not far from where he lived.'

'Why, outside in a lane, why not at his home? What took the poor lad outside in the freezing cold, and into a lane to shoot himself?'

Brenton snapped, 'how should we know, that's what happened.'

The Inspector was like a dog with a toy, he wouldn't let go. 'Give me the address of the police officer, and the address of the Clone family he wanted to protect.' He started leaving but came back partially into the room. 'You reported the Clones were afraid and being attacked. I want all the reports Clones filed on all those incidents, and what follow up you did.'

He was angry and stormed out muttering. 'About time I paid a visit to the Huxley Mayor.'

Alden knew he was making enemies, but it would bring results. He was hungry and went back to the hotel to have a shower and went down to the dining room. Josie wasn't there, when she didn't come in to serve on the dining tables, he became worried and asked after her. No one had seen her since she went to lunch. He ordered a glass of wine, but didn't wait for it, he went back to his room and tried to phone her but no answer. He knew he shouldn't go to her room but hurried there. Surely, she couldn't have been foolish enough to get involved with Stormy knowing how dangerous he was. He tapped on her door lightly, didn't get any response so tried the door, it opened. Soon as he entered the room, he could hear a disturbance in the bathroom, he went to there and saw John Hislop with his hands around Josies' neck. His reflexes were swift, he gave him a hard karate chop on the side of his neck making him slump to the floor. Josie was gasping for breath. He picked her up and placed her on her bed. She had blood all over her face and body.

John groaned. 'Where are your handcuffs?' Josie pointed to the bedside cabinet where he found her handcuffs, which he put on the semi-conscious man's hands behind his back. Alden quickly packed up all of Josie's clothing, swept his hands over what she had on her bedside cabinet into her bag. He phoned the police station. Jerry Nelson answered the phone.

'This is Inspector Miller, there is a handcuffed man, by name of John Hislop in room 305 in the Huxley Hotel, come and pick him up, put him in jail and book him for causing grievous bodily harm and attempted murder. I caught him in the act of trying to kill Josie Palmer. I want photos taken of the bedroom and the whole room cordoned off. Do it now!' After taking photos of Josies injuries, he phoned Emmitt Benson to tell him what happened, went to his house and left her in the care of Mazie and Trace Carver without stopping. Inspector Miller went straight back to the hotel, didn't see a police car outside, there was no one in her room, but it was cordoned off so went back sat at his table and glass of wine, apologized for being delayed and ordered a meal. That evening he phoned Chief Inspector Little and gave him an update.

'The reinforcements are on their way Alden, should be there by tomorrow sometime. Grateful to hear Josie is in a safe place where kind people will look after her.'

In the morning Inspector Miller went down to get another quick breakfast, he knew what he was doing, he intended to ruffle more feathers, he also knew he was putting himself in danger but was relying on help arriving.

After phoning to see how Josie was, he went straight to the Mayor's Office at the Town Hall at 8.30am, brushing straight past the receptionist who tried to get in his way and went into his office. He was aware he would have been warned about his visit, all the better, he would keep all the main players rattled. He didn't bother with pleasantries it was too late for that. He stood in front of Mayor Kingsley's desk, 'my name is Inspector Miller, and I want answers. What have you been doing to help keep order in this town when you were informed that so many of your residents had been attacked, and were being terrorized by criminals?'

The Mayor put on a brave face. 'I assure you I have done all I can to see that order has been maintained at all times.'

'Well, you haven't done a very good job Mayor, criminals are running your town.' He didn't wait for a reply. 'This concert that was here in Huxley the night the Clones disappeared, I believe you arranged it, even gave tickets to the local police so they would be there leaving a very young inexperience officer in charge of the police station. I also heard it was a very loud concert, and as so many residents where there, they say they did not hear or see anything. Very convenient.'

Inspector Miller abruptly departed, leaving Mayor Kingsley spluttering in indignation trying to defend himself.

Next call he went to see the owner of the shop that had been burnt out on High Steet. He found the owner in the shop in a back storage room, she was extremely nervous and didn't want to talk to him. 'Mrs Grey I haven't come here to cause you discomfort, all I want is the answer to a few questions. What caused the fire?'

'I believe it was a Molotov Cocktail or that's what I call them. I was working here late during the evening when someone threw one into the shop next door, the fire quickly spread to my business, I phoned the fire station and reported it.'

'Who did you speak to, and how long did they take to respond to your call?'

I spoke to Chad Wiley he is the Chief Fireman at the fire station, he said he would get here as soon as possible.'

'And did he?'

'No, by the time he got here, my shop and contents were well alight, and by the time the fire was extinguished most of my stock ruined, if not by fire, by water and smoke.'

‘How long did it take for the fire to be brought under control?’ Asked Inspector Miller who was taking notes down in a small notebook.

‘Quite a long time it seemed to me at the time, and there was only himself and one other fireman present, no other members of the fire brigade were here.’

‘I hope you had insurance Mrs Grey?’

‘I did, but I still haven’t had any financial help, the insurance people came, had a look around, and I haven’t seen them since. Numerous phone calls, and emails have been ignored, what else could I expect being a part Clone.’

‘What are your plans Mrs Grey?’

‘I am tidying up my affairs best I can, and I intend to leave Huxley as soon as the tunnel is open and trains running again. Least I’m alive, but I shouldn’t be talking to you like this, as I received death threats when police came here from Sydney asking questions, I was told to keep silent.’

‘How did you get these death threats?’

'By phone calls, people yelling out in the street in front of the shop, also had some letters thrown in my letter box.'

'Have you got any of these letters still?'

'Not now, I gave two of them not burnt to the Huxley police when they came around, they said they needed them to put in their report.'

'Thank you, please let me know if you think of anything else.' He pulled out a card from his wallet and handed it to her. 'Here is my card with my mobile number on it, if you receive any more threats let me know immediately.'

Inspector Miller decided it was now time to make another call, this one to Chief Fireman Chad Wiley. He didn't expect it would give him anything to go on, but he was making a few people concerned and uncomfortable so something might give way. He would be sleeping with his gun under his pillow from now on. He decided to use the back entrance this time, as wouldn't be expected to go in that way. When inside he saw a man sitting near a small switchboard reading a magazine who jumped in surprise when spoken to.

'Where's Chief Fireman Chad Wiley?'

The man dropped his magazine on the floor, 'he's not here?'

'Where is he, and who are you?'

'I'm Eddie. What do you want, can I help you?'

'No, you can't. Where's your boss? I want to speak to him now, my name is Inspector Miller from Sydney. Do you know what happened to the Clones who disappeared?'

Eddie remained calm just staring at him. He then looked upwards and yelled out, 'Chad you better get down here, a policeman wants to talk to you.'

Chad Wiley slid down the fireman's pole looking disheveled, and not in a good humor.

'Sorry to interrupt your nap Chad', he said sarcastically, eyeing him all over.

Chad ignored the bait. 'What do you want? I've already made my report about the night the Clones disappeared. There's nothing to add.'

'Why did you take so long to get to the fire in High Street when you received a report a fire had started next door to a business there?' This question brought a worried reaction as wasn't expected. 'What's more why only yourself, and another fireman tried to put the fire out. Why didn't you put the alarm out to gather more firemen to assist. By the time you arrived the fire was well advanced, and the person who owned the shop has lost almost all her stock and is still waiting for compensation.' Alden could see the hatred in Chad's eyes, who said nothing to defend his actions. 'How do you feel about Clones Chad, and how come you are sleeping on the job?' With that he left by the back door, but came back in again, 'and there had better not be any more death threats sent to Mrs Grey, otherwise there will be even more severe consequences coming your way.'

'Bloody hell!' Chad was furious. 'Eddie, get the Mayor on the phone straight away. This upstart is going to have to go, he's trouble.'

'The lines busy,' said Eddie.

The Mayor was on the phone, 'what do you mean, Brenton? Why is he in jail? I've got a job for him and Stormy. Get him out!'

'I was told by that Inspector to put him in, lock him up, and book him for beating up that new bar maid over at the hotel, which I might add he did a damn good job, there was blood everywhere, it's a wonder she's still alive, and for attempted murder. My hands are tied. He was a witness, saw him trying to throttle her.' and added, 'told us to cordon off the room and take photos of the blood everywhere and the bathroom.'

'Where is the bloody bitch! We must keep her quiet.' Silence.

'Brenton, where is she?'

'Don't know Mayor, when we got to the hotel she was gone, we haven't been able to locate her.'

Stormy was woken up by someone loudly banging on his door. 'Stormy it's Jake, and Clive, open up, something terrible has happened!'

Clive burst into his hall, 'it's dad, they've arrested him, he's in jail.'

They sat down at his kitchen table. Stormy got a bottle of Whiskey and three glasses. 'Now start at the beginning.'

'Ed, Jake and I have been at the pub all afternoon, playing darts and drinking, nothing else to do when it's snowing. Dad came in as you were sitting down with that bar maid, saw you giving her a drink, and you should have seen the look on his face. He muttered something like, *I'll get you, you filthy bitch,* or something like it. He kept staring at you both, and when you finally got up, said he had to go for a leek. We didn't take much notice, we were playing a game of darts and didn't see him come back. Later on, that Inspector chap came and sat down at one of the tables and ordered a drink, we heard him ask where the new barmaid was, and the owner said she hadn't seen her since she went to lunch.'

Stormy suddenly grabbed Clive by the collar of his jacket, 'what are you trying to tell me Clive, that your father went after Josie?' He was looking murderous.

Jake and Clive were scared. Clive started to cry. 'All I know is that the police arrived, and they took dad outside in handcuffs, he had blood all over him. I saw Ben, he was there with his camera, he always gets called up to take photos of anything the police want. I went up to him on his way out, and he said there was blood everywhere in the woman's room and bathroom, and everything was a mess.'

Stormy shook Clive, 'did he kill her Clive, is she dead?'

Clive was crying. 'I don't know, I don't know!'

Stormy let him go, fell back in his chair putting his hands over his eyes. He took them off and slowly lit a cigarette, he appeared to be thinking. 'That bitch, that bloody bitch. I really liked her, really had feelings for her, but she was only using me to see what she could find out.'

'What do you mean?' asked Jake.

How did that Inspector know where to go? He knew which room she was in and went to see if she was alright, most probably thought was with me. She must be an undercover cop. Bloody hell! Is she dead, did you see an ambulance take a body out?'

'No, we didn't see anything like that,' said Jake looking uncomfortable. 'I'm going home,' he quickly got up and went out the door.

The phone rang. Stormy answered, 'yes, I've just heard Mayor. Is she alive? Where is she? Bloody hell, what do you mean you don't know. You're telling me Miller saw John trying to kill her! Bloody hell, we have got to get him out of there.' He slammed the phone down. 'Clive we're going to have to get your father out before he blows the whole thing up. I know a good place where we can hide him, but I don't know the mountains as well as you do. Could you take us up to one of the huts in the gold mining area?'

'I've got a vague idea where they are, but I couldn't find them in this weather. They are completely snow bound. Dad knows where they are, he could get you there, but it's too difficult now.'

'Well, it might be the only chance of saving us all. We have to come up with an escape plan. We can't afford leaving your dad in jail. That Inspector chap is no fool. He could get him to crack if he questions him over and over, he will slip up. Let's go and pay Brenton and Jerry a visit at the police station.'

Stormy had been thinking of getting John out of the way ever since they had both been to the Trading Post, he decided to wait for the weather to improve. This latest incident was forcing him to bring things forward. He would get rid of two problems at once, John would have an accident on the way back, and the girl would never be found. The police would have no witnesses. He was not worried about the old miner. His boys in the town were seasoned criminals, they would never talk, they were happy with the way things were, and none of them had any intention of going back to prison.

Brenton was on duty by himself when they arrived. 'I was just going to phone you. Been busy doing all the paperwork booking your dad Clive and making out a report as Miller will be back to question him, and I have to cover myself. That Inspector is nothing but trouble.'

‘How’s dad?’

‘We had to clean him up, he’s out cold. Acted crazy bringing him in. He will sleep it off, the Inspector won’t be able to get any sense out of him until he wakes up.’

‘I’ll make it short,’ said Stormy, ‘we must get him out of here by tomorrow morning. Clive and I have a few arrangements to see to first.’

‘What possible reason can I give that cop if he isn’t here when he comes to question him?’

‘He’s going to break out Brenton, so you will be in the clear, but how are we going to do it?’

Brenton was thoughtful. ‘Jerry will be on duty first thing. I’ll get him to take some breakfast in, and he can let John out the back door, you be ready to pick him up. I’ll get Jerry to scatter the food everywhere, and he can say he thought John was asleep, but he jumped on him when he brought his food in knocking him to the floor and he ran outside. He would say he couldn’t leave the police station to find him but didn’t expect he would get far in this weather, and that he had phoned me, and I was on my way to look for him. How’s that sound?’

'Best we can do,' agreed Stormy, 'Clive will be waiting outside to pick him up, and I will work out the details, and where we are going to take him.'

'Where are you going to hide him?'

'That's going to be my secret, I'm closing the door on all this trouble, no more leaks.' Outside Stormy said, 'Clive we will need provisions for the trip up the mountains, it's your fathers only chance, otherwise he will go to prison for a long time for attempted murder, let alone beating that woman up, more like torturing her by the sound of things. I saw this side of him when we started killing the Clones, he was enjoying it and playing with them before he shot them and threw them over the cliff laughing, he even dangled one small girl over the side, the mother was screaming, he just dropped her down alive. I had to shoot the mother and throw her over. The child might not have died when she got to the bottom and might have been down there injured with all those dead bodies.'

Clive looked horrified, 'I know, it came out a few times as I was growing up, that's why mum left. When he didn't get what he wanted he would beat her up really bad. He nearly killed her one time, so she left soon as she was able to walk again.'

‘Why didn’t she take you with her knowing what he was like?’

‘He has never laid a hand on me, not once. He seems to hate women.’

‘I will need to talk to your dad after you pick him up in the morning, but for now we are going back to your place to get one of his unmarked vans and fill it with warm clothes, and as much food that you have on hand that doesn’t need cooking. Also, some blankets might come in handy.’

‘What about rifles?’

‘I’ll take one of John’s, that enough.’

Next morning, Clive was waiting at the back of the police station. His father came out looking dazed in the sunshine, quickly got in and laid down out of sight in the back of the van. On the way Clive explained what Stormy was planning. When back at his home, John pushed Stormy hard in the middle of his chest straight away, ‘why didn’t you tell me you knew where the girl was, you bastard?’

‘Because I wasn’t sure, and the lady at the Trading Post told me was too late to go up to the old gold mine area as snowed in, and I wanted to help you get your property business fixed up first. The girl wasn't going anywhere.'

John was mollified, he calmed down, 'guess that's right, but as soon as we get back no more waiting, I'm going into the lawyer's house and kill anyone still left there. Is that understood?'

There was no mention of Josie, it was as though she didn't exist and that he hadn't tried to kill her.

'Yeah, yeah, sure, that's understood,' said Stormy, but was thinking John was acting crazy, 'we will work it out when this business is taken care of first.'

John said, 'come with me I want to show you something.' He took them to a larger back shed, and to their surprise in a corner he uncovered a snow-mobile, the back had been extended with another seat on it. 'This might come in handy, it will fit into the back of the van, when we can't go any further, we will hide the van best we can and will travel on this, we can go up the rest of the way in no time. Just need to take some extra juice to get back.' He turned suddenly to face Stormy, 'what are we going to do with the body?'

'I've got two things worked out, we can shoot the girl, then shoot the old miner in the head with his own gun and leave him there with his gun in his hand. It will look like suicide. Or the girl must have stumbled there from where we killed the other Clones,' said Stormy 'why can't we take them back and throw them down with the others?'

John looked pleased, 'yes, that second idea is best, I didn't think about the miner's log huts, thought they would be complete ruins by now when we were looking for her. It's been years since anyone up there.' He looked around anxiously. 'Let's get going.'

Stormy thought yes, two problems taken care of at the one time. He felt sure he could get back alone on the snow mobile which he would hide when the deed was done. Clive would not be expecting to see his father, he would think he went away to escape from the law who would be looking for him as soon as the snow started to melt, he would be told the girl was dead and buried with the others.

Clive pulled Stormy back before he went to join his father in the van, he had tears in his eyes. 'You will look after dad won't you? I mean, I don't want him to suffer or anything Stormy, don't shoot him, please don't shoot him, just leave him out in the snow. He will freeze and when they find him, they will think he just died trying to get away, but it was too hard for him in the deep snow.'

Stormy realized he had understood what was going to happen. He put his hand on Clive's shoulder and silently nodded, got into the driver's seat and they drove off.

Starr was depressed. She went over the events of that terrible night again and again. She remembered her father had asked her if Heath was at the Hospital Shelter as it would be the safest place for him to be. At the time she felt happy he was accepting her relationship and was concerned for his safety, but he told her not to go there that night as mother was not feeling well, and he wanted her at home. She decided she would go to the shelter the next day, but there was no next day. Since that night her father was very caring, kind and gentle with her, but deep down she knew. She didn't want to accept he had something to do with Heaths' disappearance. Her beloved Heath would never go away without her he would have told her if there were any plans for the Clones going away. Did her father have anything to do with the Clones disappearance? He had gone out late that night when he thought she was asleep. Occasionally one or two of his new friends came to see him. Sometimes that dreadful man John Hislop came or his friend Stormy. They would have a few drinks together in the kitchen. Starr would serve the drinks and then leave, but listened behind the door hoping to hear anything that would confirm her fears. In her room this night alone with her thoughts she heard her father talking quietly, she had not heard anyone come inside, she went to listen outside the kitchen. Her father was talking. 'Don't like the sound of this, all the other Investigators were useless, this one's different and trouble. Glad you gave me the warning as he might come around here asking questions.' He was quiet listening to someone else. 'You leave my daughter out of this, she doesn't know anything, and I will never talk. I think she may suspect I had some involvement but can't prove anything. She's very depressed, but will get over it, it takes time. Best thing I ever did was getting rid of her Clone. I really enjoyed blasting his head off when I eventually found him. If I'd taken my knife I would have cut him up in pieces. Better not have you or any of the lads around while that Inspector chap is here in Huxley.'

Starr felt faint, she struggled back to her room. When she heard her father snoring and was sound asleep Starr left the house, she had packed a backpack and knew she would never be back. She couldn't stop shaking, but gradually steadied as she walked towards Emmitt Bensons' house, she had heard about him, felt she could trust him, she didn't know where else to go.

Daniel was on his way back to his parents hiding place. He had been talking with Emmitt and the family at his house, planning what they would do when the expected help arrived from Sydney. He connected the electric shock lines around the outside of Emmitt's home before he left. He was walking as could get into his family hiding place easily by losing himself in the bush roadside. He was surprised to see a young woman heading towards the home he had rigged. He went up behind the back of her, put his hand over her mouth and pulled her into the trees by the lane. 'Be quiet, I'm not going to hurt you. I'm a friend of Emmitt Benson, why are you going there?' The woman struggled. 'I'm not going to hurt you, I have to tell you the home is dangerous,' he took his hand off her mouth and let her go.

'What do you mean it is dangerous? I must go there as I've nowhere else to go. I'm desperate, my father is a killer and if his criminal friends find me, they will kill me too.'

'My name is Daniel, my mother and father and I are Clones, and we have a hiding place, my parents can look after you.' Daniel made a phone call explaining the situation. 'Dad, can I bring her to hide with us? Emmitt has more than enough people to stay with him at this time. She says her father is a killer, it might lead to concrete evidence

Inspector Miller is needing? We will be there soon.' Turning to her he asked, 'what is your name, and what is your fathers' name?'

'My name is Starr, and my father is Joe Waverly.'

'Starr come with me, you can trust me,' he said reassuringly, 'my parents want to talk to you, and we will hide you.'

At the hideaway, R630 and H200 gave Starr a warm welcome, she felt she could tell them her suspicions of her father's involvement in Heaths disappearance. 'My mother and father didn't want me to have a Clone for a boyfriend. I tried to get them to meet him, they refused. Heath and I love each other and were considering going away to live together. My father was against me leaving home. On that terrible night my father asked me if Heath was at the Hospital Shelter as he said was the safest place for him to be, he asked me not to go there as mother was not well, and he needed me at home. I heard him go out very late that night, and of course next day I wanted to go to Heath, but my father wouldn't let me leave the house as he said something terrible had happened to the Clones.' She continued, 'I knew he had something to do with this terrible business, and I have been trying to find out something every time one of those criminal types have been coming to our house since then, but it was only late tonight that I heard him talking to someone in our kitchen saying something about being warned. Something has happened, he didn't want anyone coming to our house again, and I definitely heard him say they were to leave me alone, that I didn't know anything, that I was very depressed because of that 'Clone,' and getting rid of that 'Clone' was the best thing he ever did,' she burst into tears.

Daniel felt sorry for Starr, he and his father looked at each other, perhaps this news was a piece of evidence that might lead to what had happened to the Clones. Daniel talked to his father when Starr was shown her bedroom by his mother. 'Dad I will phone Inspector Miller early tomorrow and tell him what Starr heard.'

'That might put some men in jail Daniel, but don't think they can be kept there for long without stronger evidence.'

'That could take some time dad, the town is partly guilty, they were encouraged to let it happen. The people running Huxley have let us down, we don't know yet just how many are taking bribes and who is involved with the shame of what has happened here. Huxley will always be associated with this terrible crime, and where are the bodies? Until we know that they can be arrested but can't be prosecuted, we need a witness.'

'Those poor souls, I keep seeing them in my dreams,' said H200, 'how terrified they must have been. We must find them and give them a proper memorial and get the reporters out here soon as possible. This story will have to go global. The shame is on anyone who doesn't do anything to stop this happening again.'

Daniel was on the phone talking to Inspector Miller who was in his hotel room. 'I wanted to phone you early before your colleagues get here as I know things will be busy.' He told him what had happened the night before.

'I think Starr has given us valuable information, that her father was responsible for the death of one of the Clone's, and if that was the case he was there and knows who the others are. The fact that John Hislop, Stormy and other criminal friends have been coming to see him socially since that night means he's in the middle of it. This is very good information Daniel. It might lead to arrests and where the bodies are, but it's not enough of course, but solid confirmation that Starr's father is involved. I've had a message that reinforcements are not far away. We will be having a meeting soon as they get here and be putting a plan in place. I am going to the Police Station soon as I've had a quick breakfast as I want to question John Hislop. I was told he was acting crazy and drunk, so now he has had a sleep I should be able to get something out of him. I want to question him early before he is fully awake so he might slip up, I intend to keep at him, as now positive he is one of the ring leaders in this affair.'

'Take care of yourself Inspector, let me know if I can help in any way. I saw Josie when Trace and her mother were helping her walk from the bathroom up the stairs. She was in a terrible state, the women said the bathwater was red with blood. That monster gave her a proper going over poor thing, Thank goodness you arrived in time, she is lucky to be alive.'

Stormy managed to drive a reasonable distance in the van with chains on the wheels but eventually had to leave the van at the back of an unused farmhouse where they decided to camp for the night to get some rest before getting an early start the following morning. Next day they put a few essentials in the side bags of the snow mobile and set off for the gold mining area. It had snowed again during the night, but John weaved in and out around the trees with ease over the deep snow. Finally, he came to a stop, 'this is where the early gold was found, and there were log cabins scattered up and down this valley. As I thought, can't see anything as most all in ruins covered by the snow. We must go further up the hill where we can look down, will be easier to see if anything still standing. 'Look smoke behind those trees down there.'

At the source of the smoke, there was a snug small log cabin that looked very inviting in the cold weather. Stormy just wanted to go inside, warm his hands and have something hot to drink.

Igor was content smoking his pipe, with Zoloto near-by taking out damper from the hot oven. He was hungry and looking forward to his damper and strong coffee. Oskar suddenly arose, gave a short bark and went to the door. Igor put his pipe down slowly, went to the door to put on his lambskin coat, reached for his rifle and opened the door when it suddenly burst in on him throwing him to the floor. Two men came in one had a rifle aiming straight down at him. Zoloto dropped the spatula with the damper on it and screamed. Oskar went for them teeth barred and growling. John shot the animal before it reached him. John looked at the girl with loathing, 'you bitch you have caused nothing but trouble, shut up and get us something to eat and drink, and then we are going for a walk.' She didn't hear, she was down on her knees with her arms around the dog's neck crying. John roughly pulled her away, and shook her, 'get us something to eat.'

Igor got up, 'I will get you something to eat.' He busied himself with picking up the damper, breaking it up into smaller pieces, he added some slices of cheese and cold meat giving them a plate each, which they ate greedily. Handing them a glass of Vodka he said, 'what do you want, I have no money, or anything of value?'

The two men looked at each other, the question was met with silence, Igor knew it had something to do with the girl and that she was a Clone. He didn't like the way one of them kept looking at Zoloto, who once again had retreated into herself. She was now the same as when she first came to the hut.

The angry man with the rifle pushed Zoloto, 'get outside we are going for a walk.' Igor grabbed their coats and boots before they started up the hill. Stormy took the miner's rifle and walked behind them. Igor was desperately thinking he had to do something to save her. He was an old man, if he managed to stop them so she could get away, where would she go? She did not know how to survive in the winter mountains besides she was suffering, remembering the night she ran away from another nightmare, and was reliving that trauma.

Igo stopped as he was walking up the steep mountain alongside the cabin. 'I can't go on anymore, I am an old man and need to rest,' he bent over holding his stomach.

John said, 'get moving you will have plenty of time to rest later. You know these mountains, there is a track under the snow somewhere here that leads up to a clearing that has two high rocks near a narrow road that have a split in the middle that goes down into a gully, take us there.'

Igor stretched out his hands, 'help me Zoloto,' when she came near he whispered, 'going up to the top near the clearing I'm going to try and run away, you will be on the road he is talking about, turn left to follow it to a larger road and turn left again and go down the mountain.' She just looked at him blankly. Almost at the top of the hill Igor suddenly jumped into the side trees and disappeared. John swore, he sent a few rifle shots into the area where he had gone. Zoloto screamed, she became crazy. Stormy was not sure what to do it had happened so fast.

'John, stop shooting the girl is going crazy. We can't kill them here, we can't carry both of them, it will be too difficult as we are still not sure how far we have to go.'

John wasn't listening, he ran after the old miner shooting his rifle. He went off the side of the mountain, tripped and fell hitting his head on a rock.

Stormy lent down and slapped his face, he wasn't sure if he was unconscious or dead. He decided to leave him, as he had been wondering how he was going to get rid of him, and this would save him the trouble. As he straightened up, he saw the old miner with John's rifle pointing it straight at him. Before he could pick up the miner's rifle he had placed by the rock, Igor fired but missed as Stormy rolled over. Stormy tried to grab the rifle from him and a struggle ensued, the rifle went off and Igor slumped down into the snow. Stormy had not intended to shoot him before they were where the Clones had been murdered, it was an accident. He had to think quickly, he was feeling very cold. He didn't know where the Clone burial place was, he could wander around with this crazy girl and end up dead. If he was on the main road they had travelled on, getting up to the turn-off lane he would know where he was, but he was completely lost. By leaving the two bodies there with John's rifle, it would look like John had killed him while trying to get away. He would not be involved, there would be no evidence of him being there. The girl was now still and silent, he believed her mind was affected so wouldn't be able to say anything about what happened, he had no other option but to take her back to the hut as he could see the smoke from where he was. Back at the hut he drank some Vodka and felt warmer, the girl was kneeling on the floor with her arms around the dog again. He could just leave her here, she would eventually run out of supplies and die as couldn't look after herself properly in her condition, or if anyone found her or worse if she got her memory back. He could just shoot her. No, he would have to take her back, he had no other choice. He made sure there was nothing that would show his presence there, took her outside and down to the snow mobile and made her get on the back. She was totally passive as if prepared to die. He couldn't do it, where could he hide her, how could he explain she was with him. He took her back to the hut, she had enough food and water until she was found. He drove off without her. After he had not gone far he stopped again and returned, he needed to think things out, something was wrong, he had changed in some way. He decided to return to Huxley the next day.

Inspector Miller was having a busy time at the police station with the officers who had come up to Huxley to help him. The first thing he did was get them together for a briefing of the situation and what had to be done. He had decided to use the local church hall as his headquarters as the police station was too small and needed for usual police business. He had trained officers here to help with the Clone massacre work. 'I would like to thank everyone for volunteering to come all this way to Huxley to clear up this case. We are going to work in pairs, no one is to go out alone at any time as there are some unknown criminals here, and it's going to take time to round them all up.' He paused, 'your Chief of operations will be working with me at these headquarters. Chief, give your officers their orders.'

'Right, you two go to the Mayor's office, and bring him in and the Deputy Mayor for questioning.' He handed a pair their paper, 'everything is on there where to find them and their names. Right, you two, handing them their paper, 'your job will be to pick up the Chief Fireman and his side kick, the Inspector says are arrogant and cocky, they might give you trouble so be prepared, you might need your handcuffs for those two. Now, you're next here are the names of the two police officers who have been suspended from duty, they were told to stay at home. You two will go to the Huxley Hospital and get the Principal,' handed them their paper. 'Don't take any excuses about why he can't leave his responsibilities he has 24 hours to arrange his work. Chief smiled a wide grin, 'don't say anything, but he is going to get locked up as we already have evidence against him from Doctor Dana Bentlee, it's all in her report.' Handing another paper out to another pair, 'go pick up Joe Waverley, he is one we have reasonable evidence that he killed one of the Clones.' Chief laughed, 'Awh!! There are times I really enjoy my job, there will be chairs along the hall outside this room, they can sit there while waiting their turn when they come in.'

'I need one more officer,' said Inspector Miller, 'one officer is to stand guard at Mrs Grey's shop that got burnt out in High Street or at her home, wherever she is I want a guard outside or with her, she is not to be left alone, she has had death threats from the criminals here to keep her from speaking to the authorities.'

'Chief, stay here, I'm going out to find the two ring leaders now, and they can sit in jail until we can get to them. A criminal called Stormy who has a record, and John Hislop, a well-known Clone hater and escaped prisoner who has already managed to break out of jail this morning and is on the run, he almost strangled one of our colleagues Josie Palmer who is on the mend thank God. Those that didn't get a paper will come with me as these are dangerous criminals. We will look for them both at Stormy's home first, they could be hiding there, also thoroughly go over John Hislop's home and even the two disgraced policemen's homes, he has to be somewhere here in Huxley, he can't go anywhere.'

One of the officers spoke up, 'Chief even if all these suspects are brought in or come in, you can't question them without they have a lawyer present.'

'Quite right, Chief Inspector Little has arranged for lawyers to take care of this until they get to Sydney, they should be here at any time.'

Getting ready to go out Inspector Miller strapped his gun on. Chief looked at him puzzled, 'why didn't you say anything about us having to find the bodies of the Clones, otherwise the people responsible might be jailed for taking away the homes and property but not murder?'

The police officer assigned to guard Mrs Grey went to her address, not finding her there went to her shop in High Street. He knocked on the front entrance but no answer, so called out. 'Mrs Grey I'm a police officer, and I have been given the task of guarding you.' A small face partly appeared around a wall at the back of the shop, when she saw he was a policeman she came out to speak to him.

'Inspector Miller sent you?'

'Yes, I have been assigned to be here with you. May I come inside and sit down near the front window, it's very cold out-side.'

'Of course,' she unlocked the door and let him in.

'Is there a back entrance Mrs Grey?'

She unlocked a back door, he went outside and had a look around a small courtyard, with a door to a toilet and wash basin at one end.

'It says on your report that you think a Molotov Cocktail was thrown into the shop next door. What made you think that?'

'Well, you see it in the movies, that people throw a bottle into a window and it goes off like a bomb, it's got petrol or kerosene in it or something, so I just assumed it was something like that. There was a terrible noise of the front window being smashed. It caused a terrible blaze and started coming through into my shop very quickly.'

The officer went into the shop next door through the back courtyard of the burnt-out shop. He looked everywhere but everything was blackened and damaged. On his way out he saw some glass and carefully picked up the edge a piece of thick glass from the bottom of a bottle, smelt it, carefully went back to Mrs Grey who put it into a paper bag she had in her storeroom.

As expected, Chad Wiley the Chief Fireman and his deputy Eddie were looking confident and arrogantly sure they didn't have anything to worry about as Inspector Miller and Chief come in to question them. 'To save you the trouble of lying to me, and taking up precious time as we have a lot of people to interview,' he passed over to each a sheet of paper, 'here is the time it should take to respond to a fire that was less than 10 minutes away from your Station, but you took 40 mins to get there and there is no evidence that you tried to get any other fire volunteer to come to the scene to assist. Arriving so late after being informed by the caller the fire was already coming into her shop, it appears you deliberately delayed going to the scene. Chad Wiley and you Eddie who was on duty that same evening, are both fired as from now for failing in your duty.'

'You can't do that' said Chad shocked.

'We can and have, also you were sleeping on the job during the day. He handed over another piece of paper to both men. Seems that even though you have had the same amounts of wages put into your bank accounts, we have proof that you both, especially you Chad have been doing some very heavy spending lately.'

'So, that's not against the law!'

'Seems your neighbors and friends have wondered why you have had new furniture, white goods, TVs, a scooter, expensive luxury motor bike, delivered recently. Well, I won't go on. This has been followed up, seems quite a haul, and stores around here all surprised you both paid cash for all you, and your wife's purchases. You have been taking bribes. The goods are going to be taken away. There is going to be a court case against you for taking bribes and neglection of duty.'

Chad got up angry. 'You can't do this!'

'Speak to your lawyer. His job is to advise you. This interview is over.' Chief stated the time the interview ended and turned off the machine. They walked away.

Inspector Miller with Chief were interviewing Ray Kingsley the Mayor of Huxley in the presence of a lawyer in the church hall. 'It seems that you gave Brenton Ridge free tickets for him and his wife to go to a concert which you organized, a very loud concert. Why did you do that? Looking at his roster we can see he was on duty that night. Andrew Bishop took over Brenton Ridge's shift. This meant both senior officers were at your noisy concert, and Andrew Bishop was out of the way at the police station. He couldn't go anywhere or perhaps see anything, and the other two officers had a perfect alibi that they were at the concert and didn't see or hear anything. Very convenient for you Mayor.' He shot the question out, 'who asked you to do this, or was it your idea as you were getting well paid to arrange it?'

'You are just making all this up because you haven't got anything else to go on. The concert had been on my mind for some time, the town needed to be put on the map, especially while the ski season is on. It was good for business. The police have been doing a great job here, there is nothing wrong with giving them a reward for their hard work. I wanted them to know I appreciated their efforts.'

Inspector handed him a sheet out of a folder that he had in front of him. 'Perhaps you might like to explain why you have been spending money on quite a few expensive luxuries the last few weeks. This is your bank statement, which shows your usual wages and expenses, it's certainly not enough to cover your new car which is the latest sports model. Where did you get the money?'

'A rich relative in my wife's family died and she was left a good inheritance.'

'We will check this information,' said Chief.

Ray Kingsley turned to his lawyer. 'Do I have to give my wife's personal information to the police? Her relative lived overseas. I don't know anything about them.'

'Let me remind you Mayor,' said Inspector Miller, 'that this is a murder enquiry.'

Inspector Miller and Chief were Interviewing police officer Brenton Ridge at the church hall in the presence of a lawyer. 'So, the Mayor gave you free tickets for the concert he organized, why would he do that? Very convenient to give both senior officers an alibi and leave your new young inexperienced officer on night duty out of the way.' There was no answer. 'You state in your report that he was going out with a young Clone that he had rescued from attackers.' He picked up another folder and looked inside. 'According to Andrew Bishop's report, after hearing from you next day that the Clones had disappeared, he went to her home and there was no sign of the young woman or her mother. It was also in his report, that a neighbor and two of her friends were stealing their belongings when he went there to find them. He also made a report that a neighbor living in the same street saw the two women walking up the lane at the back of her house late at night in the direction of the Hospital Shelter, they had a torch so they could see where they were walking, she saw them clearly.'

Chief said, 'why was there no report of follow up to get the stolen property back from these three women?'

Brenton was just staring at them arrogantly with his arms folded.

Miller continued, 'also in a previous report he wrote that he was told it was a waste of time reporting anything to the police because no action was ever taken if you were a Clone. Andrew Bishop went to the hospital, and no one would talk to him about what happened. No one saw anything or heard anything. He received the same response from all others he tried to interview throughout the day. It's no wonder he was depressed, feeling guilty that he had not done enough to get them to safety with so much hatred in the town. He got drunk went to the lane where they were last seen, that was why he was there.'

'You didn't write a report on the suicide scene, only one photo of the dead police officer on the ground with his gun near him,' said Chief.

'What was there to report, he shot himself.' Brenton replied.

'I expect he found something that belonged to her,' said Inspector Miller, 'looks like there is a scarf hanging out of his pocket. So, as he couldn't handle the emotions and had no one to turn to that he could rely on, he shot himself,' said Miller. 'Why didn't you follow up reports of Clones being attacked, and their property being stolen? I'll tell you why, you hate Clones and you were taking bribes!'

Brenton gave his lawyer a questioning look, who said, 'don't say anything.'

'You can't prove anything.'

'You're a disgrace to the force, and we will see to it that you never wear a police uniform again,' said Chief.

Inspector Miller and Chief were just about to interview the Hospital Principal who had been waiting outside in the hall, when two policemen walked in. 'Chief, we have been looking for John Hislop at his home, couldn't find him anywhere, so got his son to unlock his back shed and we found around twenty Molotov Cocktails all made up on a bench ready for use. His son Clive said he had nothing to do with making them, and as usual doesn't know why they are there, and doesn't have any idea where his father is. Said he hadn't been home since he broke out of jail. We left everything as it is, locked up the shed and we have the key.'

'Well,' said Chief, if any of the bottles is the same glass as the one brought in from the fire scene in High Street, we have evidence who was responsible for causing that fire.'

The Principal of the Huxley Hospital was looking very nervous as they came to question him.

Inspector Miller didn't waste any time, he disliked the man because of what he heard from Doctor Bentlee, he tried not to show it.

'On the night the Clones disappeared where were you?'

'I was at home, I am not usually at the hospital in the evenings unless I am called in by one of the doctors, my job is purely an administrator. I run the hospital from my office, staff come to me.'

'What procedures did you follow when you realized the Clones were no longer there? What enquiries did you make?'

'There was no procedure to follow, nothing like this had ever happened before, but naturally I interviewed all staff that were on duty that night.'

'What was the outcome of these interviews?'

'That the staff were locked into two rooms, they didn't know by whom as the people had their faces covered. There was a lot of noise and talking, and when all quiet some patients let them out. They saw nothing that helped me understand what had happened, but one or two patients suggested that the Clones had been planning to get away from Huxley for some time, as there was a lot of ill feeling towards them because of the way they were affecting the local resident's livelihoods.'

'You were told that a phone call had been received that there was an armed mob on its way to the hospital?'

'I was not informed of any such phone call.'

'So why did most of the night staff hurriedly leave the hospital?'

'They did not.'

'And just where do you think the Clones would have gone Principal?'

'I have no idea where? Obviously, there was some plan that's why there were so many who came to this one place to be together, they had arranged to be picked up and taken away.'

Inspector Miller changed his questioning. 'Why did you take Doctor Bentlee away from her home which is next to the hospital against her will after that night, then bring her back after our previous police colleagues had left to go back to Sydney, then requesting her to pack some of her belongings and tell her you were coming back the next day to take her somewhere else to live. She was in her own home, and you stated that the doctor taking her husband's position at the hospital was going to live there.'

'She was diagnosed by two of our doctors at the hospital of being mentally unfit since the disappearance of her husband to stay in that large house and look after herself. A very comfortable and suitable smaller home was to be given to her from the hospital. She was being cared for in the best possible way.'

'You knew that the property she and her husband lived in was built and belonged to her, and in fact they were responsible for the building of the Huxley Hospital years ago.'

'I knew no such thing, that is not correct.'

Inspector Miller passed over some documents, 'these documents are copies of the legal right of the Bentlee's as owners of the property, and their financial involvement building the medical complex in Huxley.'

The Principal's face turned pale. 'They are forgeries.'

'I'm afraid not Principal, in fact we have evidence that you had intended to take over the property of Doctor Bentlee as soon as you placed her elsewhere. You had already booked the local removalists to shift your belongings to her address. Who was helping you with this fraudulent activity to defraud this woman out of her rightful property? Who was giving you bribes for your silence of what happened at the hospital?'

'You are under arrest,' said Chief. He called out to a policeman waiting by the door, 'take this man away, read him his rights and put him in jail.'

Inspector Miller reached for his coat. 'Chief, it's time we go for another search over Stormy's home that he moved into that previously belonged to a missing Clone's family. He was seen leaving a day or two ago by a neighbor, hopefully he has come home. We have to find him.'

Stormy came into town the next morning from the mining area and soon became aware of the larger police presence in Huxley. He knew the law was closing in, it was only a matter of time. He had a desperate urge to see Josie again. He had to see her while he was still free, so he went straight to Emmitt's house. He went up to the front door and knocked loudly calling out, 'Emmitt it's me Stormy, I want to talk to Josie.'

Emmitt unlocked the door but stayed behind the security screen, 'what do you want, I don't think she would want to speak to you?'

Stormy called out, 'Josie, it's Stormy, I just want to speak to you, it's important.'

Josie needed Emmitt's help to get down the stairs, he was surprised to see the look on her face as she went towards the door. That look showed him she had feelings for this man who she knew was a criminal. 'I'm here Stormy, what do you want to tell me?'

'Are you feeling better Josie, I was told John beat you up badly, I should have been there, should have protected you.'

'You couldn't have known what he was going to do.'

'Josie let me see your face, it might be the last time I will get to see you. Please, I just want to see your face, I'm not here to hurt you.' He went closer to the doorway as she started to open the security door slightly. He gasped in shock at the injuries he could see. If he hadn't known John was dead, he would have gone out then and there and killed him. He lowered his voice, 'I must tell you something, my real name is William. I was nicknamed Stormy by my mates when I was young, because I was always flaring up angry, out of control all the time like a storm, it stuck,' he lent towards her,' the other thing I have to tell you Josie is that I have never been loved, nor have I ever loved anyone, but I have strong feelings for you Josie, in fact I love you. I wanted to be a better person because of you. I would have changed, but I'm in this Clone mess too deep Josie, I'm in too deep. It's too late for me. I wanted you to know I love you.' With that confession he turned away and walked down the path to a van not looking back.

Stormy went looking for Inspector Miller and found him in the church hall. He didn't expect to see Brenton or Jerry, new police officers were there now talking to the Inspector.

'I want to speak to Inspector Miller.'

Alden saw him and went to the front of the hall. Before he could say anything, Stormy looked at him straight in the eyes, 'Miller I'm turning myself in, I killed Clones from the Hospital Shelter.'

'So, you know where the bodies are Stormy?'

'Yes, and I can show you where we shot them and threw their bodies down into a crevice high up in the mountains. Also, I've got someone to leave here, she needs help, she's just outside.' Stormy went out into the hallway and came back with Zoloto.

Outside the Huxley Hotel were placards discarded along the front wall. Inside drinks were flowing freely with the victors in jubilant mood. Emmitt was in the middle surrounded by well-wishers on a successful voting campaign, as he was now the new Mayor of Huxley.

Exhausted but happy he extracted himself from the throng, joining his hardworking team sitting at a table waiting for him. 'I want to thank you all,' he touched his glass of wine with those of Daniel, H200, R630, Starr, Trace, Jax, Mazie and Sidney, and Adrianna Carver's lemonade.

'We are going to go over to our reserved table, our food will be ready soon,' said Starr.

'Go on over, Emmitt and I just need a few minutes together,' said H200.

'I just wanted to ask you Emmitt how Josie is getting on, will she be leaving soon?'

'Yes, she will. The local phycologist has been treating her, she is mentally getting over her experience, and her wounds have almost healed so physically looking better now. The same phycologist has done wonders with Zoloto, she has helped the poor girl to remember that terrible night and deal with what she saw and experienced, so she is Inspector Miller's main witness in all this terrible case. Now the train is running again the three of them will be leaving soon I expect. Other police will be remaining in Huxley to ensure there is law and order, there are a few matters to be sorted out and cleared up. There are still more arrests to be made.'

'Terrible shame about the old Russian miner, he saved the girl when she was lost, but now we know what happened to John Hislop. Stormy hasn't got a chance of ever getting out of prison. The trial will most probably go on for some time,' said H200.

'Yes, it will, but now there is the shocking job of getting the Clone bodies up and out of the crevice if possible and given a decent burial. If not, I want to arrange putting up a plaque with all their names on it. Also, I will get the remains of the old miner and his friend who is buried up there near his log hut a decent burial as well.' Emmitt sighed, 'so much to do.'

H200 repeated thoughtful, 'yes so much to do Emmitt. Why doesn't anything ever change? Why is it that in history humans follow the leaders who want to take over the rest of the world. Why aren't they content with what they have. There is something terrible in human makeup that wants to control others, possess their land and property and kill to get it. Ordinary people are the ones that suffer as they have to obey their orders. There are few bad leaders, and millions of decent people, why does this keep happening? I don't know the answer.' He was looking over at his wife R630, where he could also see that Daniel and Starr were holding hands under the table talking and laughing. 'You will be getting married to Trace very soon Emmitt?'

'We have discussed it, we would like to but somehow doesn't seem right with so much unhappiness here at present, perhaps we should wait for a few more months. I want to take Trace to Sydney to meet my parents, while there try and employ a new lawyer to come up here to work. I know two other lawyers a husband and wife team, I will approach them as well, we need them here. After seeing the improvement the phycologist made in the lives of trauma victims Josie and Zoloto, Trace is going to enroll in a Sydney University course she has seen on the internet. She would make a good phycologist.'

'That would be a wonderful career for her, and we certainly need more people in these kinds of professions, there is so much healing that needs to be done here,' said H200.

'Besides, I have to get properly settled into my new job,' said Emmitt. 'Things certainly are better in Huxley, but a lot of those living in the surrounding villages are not happy a part Clone got the position of Mayor, but things will change, they have to change.' He got up, 'let's go and join our families.'

H200 said, 'the most important things in life no matter what happens, is love and courage.'

'Yes, you are right,' said Emmitt, 'love and courage.'

Inspector Miller had one last thing to do before he left Huxley. He drove to the airport and picked up Doctor Dana Bentlee and drove her back to her home adjacent to the Huxley Hospital.

'Doctor, are you sure you are emotionally up to coming back here and working at the hospital after what happened to your husband and all the terrible events that happened here?'

'My husband will be with me in spirit. I met him when I came here, we built these facilities when there was nothing here. Scott shared my dreams and hopes for building a place where people living in such remote villages could get medical help and Clones could live in safety and freedom, that's why I became a doctor, I need to keep that dream alive, and to get back to work.'

'I wonder if you would like some company,' said Inspector Miller, 'and help someone who needs a home. I will arrange to send you her medical notes, she needs to stay here and continue the treatment she is receiving, it would not be good for her to change doctors at this stage. She is my star witness, her name is Zoloto. A young girl who is going to have to come to Sydney with you when the time comes, for the trial of all those responsible for the Clone Hospital massacres.'

About the Author

Rhonda Dolzan is an accomplished author known for her captivating novels that blend psychological intrigue with thrilling narratives. Her work often explores the complexities of human behaviour, morality, and survival in challenging circumstances.

Every story I write comes from a deep place of curiosity about people-how we think, how we act, and what we are willing to do when the stakes are high. From psychological thrillers to historical non-fiction, my books dive into the heart of human conflict. If you enjoy stories that aren't afraid to explore the dark corners of the mind, you're in the right place. My name is Rhonda Dolzan, and I'm here to share my world with you.

www.ingramcontent.com/pod-product-compliance
Lightning Source LLC
Chambersburg PA
CBHW041746010726
47507CB00008B/306

* 9 7 8 1 7 6 4 4 2 0 7 0 9 *